THE BOY WITH THE U. S. FORESTERS

FRANCIS ROLT-WHEELER

THE BOY WITH THE U. S. FORESTERS

CHAPTER I

ENTERING THE SERVICE

"Hey, Wilbur, where are you headed for?"

The boy addressed, who had just come through the swing-doors of an office building in Washington, did not slacken his pace on hearing the question, but called back over his shoulder:

"To the forest, of course. Come along, Fred."

"But—" The second speaker stopped short, and, breaking into a run, caught up with his friend in a few steps.

"You certainly seem to be in a mighty big hurry to get there," he said.

"We don't loaf on our service," answered the boy with an air of pride.

His friend broke into a broad grin. He had known Wilbur Loyle for some time, and was well aware of his enthusiastic nature.

"How long has it been 'our' service?" he queried, emphasizing the pronoun.

"Ever since I was appointed," rejoined Wilbur exultantly.

"I'm glad the appointment has had time to soak in; it didn't take long, did it?" Wilbur flushed a little, and his chum, seeing this, went on laughingly: "Don't mind my roasting, old man, only you were 'way up in the clouds."

The boy's expression cleared instantaneously, and he laughed in reply.

"I suppose I was," he said, "but it's great to feel you've got the thing you've been working for. As you know, Fred, I've been thinking of this for years; in fact, I've always wanted it, and I've worked hard to get it. And then the Chief Forester's fine; he's just fine; I liked him ever so much."

"Did you have much chance to talk with him?"

"Yes, quite a lot. I thought I was likely enough to meet him, and p'raps he would formally tell me I was appointed and then bow me out of the office. Not a bit of it. He told me all about the Service, showed me just what there was in it for the country, and I tell you what—he made me feel that I wanted to go right straight out on the street and get all the other boys to join."

"Why?"

"Well, he showed me that the Forest Service gave a fellow a chance to make good even better than in the army or the navy. There you have to follow orders mainly; there's that deadly routine besides, and you don't get much of a chance to think for yourself; but in the Forest Service a chap is holding down a place of trust where he has a show to make good by working it out for himself."

"Sounds all right," said the older boy. "Anyway, I'm glad if you're glad."

"What I like about it," went on Wilbur, "is the bigness of the whole thing and the chance a chap has to show what he's made of. Glad? You bet I'm glad!"

"You weren't so sure whether you were going to like it or not when you went in to see about it," said Fred.

"Oh, yes, I was. I knew I was going to like it all right. But I didn't know anything about where I might be sent or how I would be received."

"I think it's just ripping," said his friend, "that it looks so good to you, starting out. It makes a heap of difference, sometimes, how a thing begins."

"It surely does. Right now, the whole thing seems too good to be true."

"Well," said the other, "as long as it strikes you that way I suppose you're satisfied now for all the grind you did preparing for it. But I don't believe it would suit me. It might be all right to be a Forest Ranger, but you told me one time that you had to start in as a Fire Guard, a sort of Fire Policeman, didn't you?"

"Sure!"

"Well, that doesn't sound particularly exciting."

"Why not? What more excitement do you want than a forest fire! Isn't that big enough for you?"

3

"The fire would be all right," answered the older boy, "but it's the watching and waiting for it that would get me."

"You can't expect to have adventures every minute anywhere," said Wilbur, "but even so, you're not standing on one spot like a sailor in a crow's nest, waiting for something to happen; you're in the saddle, riding from point to point all day long, sometimes when there is a trail and sometimes when there isn't, out in the real woods, not in poky, stuffy city streets. You know, Fred, I can't stand the city; I always feel as if I couldn't breathe."

"All right, Wilbur," said the other, "it's your own lookout, I suppose. Me for the city, though."

Just then, and before Fred could make any further reply, a hand was laid on Wilbur's shoulder, and the lad, looking around, found the Chief Forester walking beside them.

"Trying to make converts already, Loyle?" he asked with a smile, nodding pleasantly to the lad's companion.

"I was trying to, sir," answered the boy, "but I don't believe Fred would ever make one of us."

The Chief Forester restrained all outward trace of amusement at the lad's unconscious coupling of the head of the service and the newest and youngest assistant, and, turning to the older boy, said questioningly:

"Why not, Fred?"

"I was just saying to Wilbur, sir," he replied in a stolid manner, "that a Forest Guard's life didn't sound particularly exciting. It might be all right when a fire came along, but I should think that it would be pretty dull waiting for it, week after week."

"Not exciting enough?" The boys were nearly taken off their feet by the energy of the speaker. "Not when every corner you turn may show you smoke on the horizon? Not when every morning finds you at a different part of the forest and you can't get there quick enough to convince yourself that everything is all right? Not when you plunge down ravines, thread your way through and over fallen timber, and make up time by a sharp

4

gallop wherever there's a clearing, knowing that every cabin you pass is depending for its safety on your care? And then that is only a small part of the work. If you can't find excitement enough in that, you can't find it in anything."

"Yes—" began Fred dubiously, but the Chief Forester continued:

"And as for the responsibility! I tell you, the forest is the place for that. We need men there, not machines. On the men in the forest millions of dollars' worth of property depends. More than that, on the care of the Forest Guards hangs perhaps the stopping of a forest fire that otherwise would ravage the countryside, kill the young forest, denude the hills of soil, choke with mud the rivers that drain the denuded territory, spoil the navigable harbors, and wreck the prosperity of all the towns and villages throughout that entire river's length."

"I hadn't realized there was so much in it," replied Fred, evidently struck with the Forester's earnestness.

"You haven't any idea of how much there is in it. Not only for the work itself, but for you. Wild horses can't drag a man out of the Service once he's got in. It has a fascination peculiarly its own. The eager expectancy of vast spaces, the thrill of adventure in riding off to parts where man seldom treads, and the magnificent independence of the frontiersman, all these become the threads of which your daily life is made."

"It sounds fine when you put it that way, sir," said Fred, his eyes kindling at the picture. "But it's hardly like that at first, is it?"

"Certainly it is! Does the life of a fireman in a big city fire department strike you as being interesting or exciting?"

"Oh, yes, sir!"

"It isn't to be compared with that of the Forest Guard. A city fireman is only one of a company huddled together in a little house, not greatly busy until the fire telegraph signal rings. But suppose there were only one fireman for the whole city, that he alone were responsible for the safety of every house, that instead of telegraphic signaling he must depend on his trusty horse to carry him to suitable vantage points, and on his eyesight when there;

suppose that he knew there was a likelihood of fire every hour out of the twenty-four, and that during the season he could be sure of two or three a week, don't you think that fireman would have a lively enough time of it?"

"He surely would," said Wilbur.

"Aside from the fact that there are not as many people involved, that's not unlike a Forest Guard's position. I tell you, he's not sitting around his shack trying to kill time." Then, turning sharply to the older boy, the Chief Forester continued:

"What do you want to be?"

"I had wanted to be a locomotive engineer, sir," was the boy's reply, "but now I think I'll stay in the city."

"It was the excitement of the life that appealed to you, was it?"

"Yes, sir. I guess so."

"True, there's a good deal of responsibility there, when you stand with your hand on the throttle of a fast express, knowing that the lives of the passengers are in your hand. There's a good deal of pride, too, in steering a vessel through a dangerous channel or in a stormy sea; there's a thrill of power when you sight a big gun and know that if you were in warfare the defense of your country might lie in your skill and aim. But none of these is greater than the sense of power and trust reposing in the men of the Forest Service, to whom Uncle Sam gives the guardianship and safe-keeping of millions of acres of his property and the lives of thousands of his citizens."

The Chief Forester watched the younger of his companions, who was striding along the Washington street, and casting rapid glances from building to building as he went along, as though he expected to see flame and smoke pouring from every window, and that the city's safety lay in his hands. Smiling slightly, very slightly, and addressing himself to the older boy, although it was for the benefit of his new assistant that he was speaking, the Forester continued:

"It's really more like the work of a trusted army scout than anything else. In the old days of Indian warfare," — both boys gave a quick start of increased attention—"the very finest men and the most to be trusted were the scouts. They were men of great bravery, of undaunted loyalty, of great wariness, and filled with the spirit of dashing adventure. They were men who took their lives in their own hands. Going before the main body of the army, single-handed, if need be, they would stave off the attacks of Indian foes and would do battle with outposts and pickets. If the force were too great, they would map out the lay of the land and devise a strategical plan of attack, then, without rest or food often, would steal back to the main body, and, laying their information in the hands of the general, would act as guides if he ordered a forward movement."

"But how—" interrupted Fred.

"I was just coming to that," replied the Forester in response to his half-uttered query. "A Forest Guard is really a Forest Scout. There have been greater massacres at the hands of the Fire Tribe than from any Indian tribe that ever roamed the prairies. Hundreds, yes, thousands of lives were lost in the days before the Forest Service was in existence by fires which Forest Scouts largely could have prevented. Why, I myself can recall seeing a fire in which nearly a thousand and a half persons perished."

"In one fire?"

"Just in one fire. What would you think if you were told that in a forest in front of you were several thousand savages, all with their war-paint on, waiting a chance to break forth on the villages of the plain, that you had been chosen for the post of honor in guarding that strip of plain, and that the lives of those near by depended on your alertness? If they had picked you out for that difficult and important post, do you think that you would go and stand your rifle up against a tree and look for some soft nice mossy bank on which to lie down and go to sleep?"

"I'd stay on the job till I dropped," answered Wilbur quickly and aggressively.

"There's really very little difference between the two positions," said the Chief Forester. "No band of painted savages can break forth from a forest with more appalling fury than can a fire, none is more difficult to resist,

7

none can carry the possibility of torture to its hapless victims more cruelly, none be so deaf to cries of mercy as a fire. Instead of keeping your ears open for a distant war-whoop, you have to keep your eyes open for the thin up-wreathing curl of smoke by day, or the red glow and flickering flame at night, which tells that the time has come for you to show what stuff you are made of. On the instant must you start for the fire, though it may be miles away, crossing, it may be, a part of the forest through which no trail has been made, plunging through streams which under less urgency would make you hesitate to try them, single-handed and 'all on your own,' to fight Uncle Sam's battles against his most dangerous and most insistent foe."

"But if you can't put it out?" suggested Fred.

"It has got to be put out," came the sharp reply, with an insistence of manner that told even more than the words. "There isn't anything else to it. If you have to get back to headquarters or send word there, if all the Rangers in the forest have to be summoned, if you have to ride to every settlement, ranch, and shack on the range, yes, if you have to rouse up half the State, this one thing is sure — the fire has got to be put out."

"But can you get help?"

"Nearly always. In the first place, the danger is mutual and everybody near the forest or in it will suffer if the fire spreads. In the second place, the Service is ready to pay men a fair wage for the time consumed in putting out a fire, and even the Ranger has the right to employ men to a limited extent. Sometimes the blaze can be stopped without great difficulty, at other times it will require all the resources available under the direction of the Forest Supervisor, but in the first resort it depends largely upon the Guard. A young fellow who is careless in such a post as that is as great a traitor to his country as a soldier would be who sold to the enemy the plans of the fort he was defending, or a sailor who left the wheel while a battle-ship was threading a narrow and rocky channel."

"What starts these forest fires, sir?" asked Fred.

"All sorts of things, but most of them arise from one common cause — carelessness. There are quite a number of instances in which fires have been started by lightning, but they are few in number as compared with those due to human agency. The old tale of fires being caused by two branches of a dead tree rubbing against each other is, of course, a fable."

"But I should think any one would know enough not to start a forest fire," exclaimed the older boy. "I'm not much on the woods, but I think I know enough for that."

"It isn't deliberate, it's careless," repeated the Forester. "Sometimes a camper leaves a little fire smoldering when he thinks the last spark is out; sometimes settlers who have to burn over their clearings allow the blaze to get away from them; when Indians are in the neighborhood they receive a large share of the blame, and the hated tramp is always quoted as a factor of mischief. In earlier days, sparks from locomotives were a constant danger, and although the railroad companies use a great many precautions now to which formerly they paid no heed, these sparks and cinders are still a prolific cause of trouble. And beside this carelessness, there is a good deal of inattention and neglect. The settlers will let a little fire burn for days unheeded, waiting for a rain to come along and put it out, whereas if a drought ensues and a high wind comes up, a fire may arise that will leap through the forest and leave them homeless, and possibly even their own lives may have to pay the penalty of their recklessness."

"But what I don't understand," said Fred, "is how people get caught. It's easy enough to see how a forest could be destroyed, but I should think that every one could get out of the way easily enough. It must take a tree a long while to burn, even after it gets alight, especially if it's a big one."

"A big forest fire, fanned by a high wind, and in the dry season," answered the Chief Forester, "could catch the fastest runner in a few minutes. The flames repeatedly have been known to overtake horses on the gallop, and where there are no other means of escape the peril is extreme."

"But will green trees burn so fast?" the older boy queried in surprise. "I should have thought they were so full of sap that they wouldn't burn at all."

"The wood and foliage of coniferous trees like spruce, fir, and pine are so full of turpentine and resin that they burn like tinder. The heat is almost beyond the power of words to express. The fire does not seem to burn in a steady manner, the flames just breathe upon an immense tree and it becomes a blackened skeleton which will burn for hours.

"The actual temperature in advance of the fire is so terrific that the woods begin to dry and to release inflammable vapors before the flames reach them, when they flash up and add their force to the fiery hurricane. It is almost unbelievable, too, the way a crown-fire will jump. Huge masses of burning gas will be hurled forth on the wind and ignite the trees two and three hundred yards distant. Fortunately, fires of this type are not common, most of the blazes one is likely to encounter being ground fires, which are principally harmful in that they destroy the forest floor."

"But I should have thought," said Wilbur, "that such fires could only get a strong hold in isolated parts where nobody lives."

"Not at all. Sometimes they begin quite close to the settlements, like the destructive fire at Hinckley, Minnesota, in 1894, which burned quietly for a week, and could have been put out by a couple of men without any trouble; but sometimes they start in the far recesses of the forest and reach their full fury very quickly. Of course, every fire, even the famous Peshtigo fire, started as a little bit of a blaze which either of you two boys could have put out."

"How big a fire was that, sir?" asked Fred.

"It covered an area of over two thousand square miles."

"Great Cæsar!" ejaculated Wilbur after a rapid calculation, "that would be a strip twenty miles wide and a hundred miles long."

The Chief Forester nodded.

"It wiped the town of Peshtigo entirely off the map," he said. "The people were hemmed in, ringed by fire on every side, and out of a population of two thousand, scarcely five hundred escaped. Flight was hopeless and rescue impossible."

"And could this have been stopped after it got a hold at all?" asked Wilbur seriously, realizing the gravity of the conditions that some day he might have to face. "Could not something have been done?"

"It could have been prevented," said the Chief Forester fiercely, "and as I said, in the first few hours either one of you boys could have put it out. But there have been many others like it since, and probably there will be many others yet to come. Even now, there are hundreds of towns and villages near forest lands utterly unprovided with adequate fire protection. Some of them are near our national forests, and it is our business to see that no danger comes to them. Think of a fire like that of Peshtigo, think that if it had been stopped at the very beginning a thousand and a half lives would have been saved, and then ask yourself whether the work of a Forest Guard is not just about as fine a thing as any young fellow can do."

Wilbur turned impulsively to his chum.

"You'll just have to join us, Fred," he said. "I don't see how any one that knows anything about it can keep out. You could go to a forestry school this summer and start right in to get ready for it."

"I'll think about it," said the older boy.

The Chief Forester was greatly pleased with the lad's eagerness to enroll his friend, and, turning to him, continued:

"I don't want you to think it's all fire-fighting in the forest, though, Loyle; so I'll give you an idea of some of the other opportunities which will come your way in forest work. I suppose both of you boys hate a bully? I know I used to when I was at school."

"I think," said Wilbur impetuously, "that a bully's just about the worst ever."

"I do, too," joined in Fred.

"Well, you'll have a chance to put down a lot of bullying. You look surprised, eh? You don't see what bullying has to do with forestry? It has, a great deal, and I'll show you how. I suppose you know that a forest is a good deal like a school?"

"Well, no," admitted Wilbur frankly, "I don't quite see how."

"A forest is made up of a lot of different kind of trees, isn't it, just as a school is made up of a lot of boys? And each of these trees has an individuality, just in the same way that each boy has an individuality. That, of course, is easy to see. But what is more important, and much less known, is that just as the school as a whole gets to have a certain standard, so does the forest as a whole."

"That seems queer," remarked Fred.

"Perhaps it does, but it's true none the less. In many schools there are some boys bigger than others, but who are not good for as much, and they're always picking at the others and crowding them down. In the same way in a forest there are always some worthless trees, trying to crowd out the ones which are of more value. As the trees of better value are always sought for their timber, that gives the worthless stuff a good chance to get ahead. One of the duties of a Forester, looking after his section of the forest, is to see that every possible chance is given to the good over the bad."

"It's really like having people to deal with!" cried Fred in surprise. "It sounds as if a tree were some kind of a human being."

"There are lots of people," said the Chief Forester, "who think of trees and speak of trees just exactly as if they were people like themselves. And it isn't even only the growing of the right kind of trees, but there are lots of ways of handling them under different conditions and at different ages. Thus, a Forester must be able to make his trees grow in height up to a certain stage, then stop their further growth upwards and make them put on diameter."

"But how can you get a tree to grow in a certain way?" asked Fred in utter amazement.

"Get Loyle here to tell you all about it. I suppose you learned that at the Ranger School, didn't you?" he added, turning to the younger boy.

"Yes, sir. We had a very interesting course in silviculture."

"But just to give you a rough idea, Fred," continued the Forester, "you know that some trees need a lot of light. Consequently, if a number of young trees are left fairly close together, they will all grow up straight as fast as they can, without putting out any branches near the bottom, and all their growth will be of height."

"See, Fred," interjected Wilbur, "that's why saplings haven't got any twigs except just at the top."

"Just so," said the Forester. "Presently," he continued, "as these young trees grow up together, one will overtop the rest. If the adjacent small trees be cut down when this tallest tree has reached a good height, it will spread at the top in order to get as much sunlight as possible. In order to carry a large top the diameter of the trunk must increase. So, by starting the trees close together and allowing one of them to develop alone after a certain height has been reached, the Forester has persuaded that tree first to grow straight and high, and then to develop girth, affording the finest and most valuable kind of lumber. That's just one small example of the scores of possibilities that lie in the hands of the expert Forester. By proper handling a forest can be made to respond to training, as I said, just as a school might do."

"I can tell you a lot more things, Fred, just as wonderful as that," commented Wilbur.

The Chief Forester nodded.

"I'd like to hear you myself," he said; "I'd rather listen to something about trees than eat. But I've got to go now. I'll see you again soon, Loyle," and with a parting good wish to both boys, he crossed the street and went on his way.

CHAPTER II

PUTTING A STOP TO GUN-PLAY

Wilbur was sitting in the writing-room of the hotel where he was staying while in Washington, just finishing a letter home telling of his good-fortune and his appointment, when a bell-boy came to tell him that his uncle, Mr. Masseth, was downstairs waiting to see him. This uncle had been a great inspiration to Wilbur, for he was prominent in the Geological Survey, and had done some wonderful work in the Canyon of the Colorado. Wilbur hurried down at once.

"Congratulations!" the geologist said, as soon as the boy appeared. "So you came through with flying colors, I hear."

"Every one was just as fine as could be," answered the lad. "But how did you know about it, uncle?"

"You wrote me that you were going to call on the Chief Forester to-day, and so I took the trouble to telephone to one of the men in the office who would be likely to know the result of your interview."

"Isn't it bully?"

"Yes," said the older man with a quiet laugh, "I think it is 'bully,' as you call it. But I didn't call only to congratulate you; I thought perhaps you would like to come with me to-night and meet some of the men in the Forest Service who are really doing things out West. If you do, there's no time to waste."

"You bet I do," the boy replied hastily. "But what is it all about?"

"It's a lecture on forestry in China, but it happens to come at the same time as a meeting of the District Foresters, so they're all in town. Trot along upstairs and get your hat, and we can talk about it on the way."

The geologist sauntered over to an acquaintance who was standing in the hotel lobby near by, but he had hardly exchanged half a dozen sentences with him when Wilbur reappeared, ready to go.

"You see," said Masseth as they left the hotel, "it is a good plan for you to meet as many of the leaders of your profession as you can, not only because their friendship may be useful to you, nor yet only because they are all pleasant fellows, but because forestry is a profession, a very large and complex one, and it is a revelation sometimes to see what can be made of it. I know myself, whenever I meet a great geologist I always feel a little better to think I can say, 'I am a geologist, too.' So you, I hope, may be able to say some day, 'I am a Forester, too.'"

"I'm one now," said Wilbur elatedly.

"You're not, you're only a cub yet," corrected his uncle sharply; "don't let your enthusiasm run away with your good sense. You are no more a Forester yet than a railroad bill-clerk is a transportation expert."

"All right, uncle," said Wilbur, "I'll swallow my medicine and take that all back. I'm not even the ghost of a Forester — yet."

"You will meet the real article to-night. As I told you, the District Foresters are East for a conference, and this lecture is given before the Forestry Association. So you will have a good chance of sizing up the sort of men you are likely to be with."

"Will the Forest Supervisors be there, too?"

"I should imagine not. There may be one or two in town. But the Supervisors alone would make quite a gathering if they were all here. There are over a hundred, are there not? You ought to know."

"Just a hundred and forty-one now — about one to each forest."

"And there are only six District Foresters?"

"Yes. One is in Montana, one in Colorado, one in New Mexico, one in Utah, one in California, and one in Oregon. And they have under their charge, so I learned to-day, nearly two hundred million acres of land, or, in other words, territory larger than the whole state of Texas and five times as large as England and Wales."

"I had forgotten the figures," said the geologist. "That gives each District Forester a little piece of land about the size of England to look after. And they can tell you, most of them, on almost every square mile of that region, approximately how much marketable standing timber may be found there, what kinds of trees are most abundant, and in what proportion, and roughly, how many feet of lumber can be cut to the acre. It's always been wonderful to me. That sort of thing takes learning, though, and you've got to dig, Wilbur, if you want to be a District Forester some day."

"I'm going to get there some day, all right."

"If you try hard enough, you may. By the way, there's one of them going in now. That's the house, on the other side of the Circle."

The boy looked across the curve and scanned all the men going in the same direction, quite with a feeling of companionship. One of the men who overtook and passed them, giving a hearty greeting to Masseth as he went by, was Roger Doughty, a young fellow who had distinguished himself in the Geological Survey, having taken a trip from south to north of Alaska, and Wilbur's companion felt a twinge of regret that his nephew had not entered his own service.

Wilbur, however, was always a "woods" boy, and even in his early childish days had been possessed with a desire to camp out. He had read every book he could lay hands on that dealt with "the great outdoors," and would ten thousand times over rather have been Daniel Boone than George Washington. Seeing his intense pleasure in that life, his father had always allowed him to go off into the wilds for his holidays, and in consequence he knew many little tricks of woodcraft and how to make himself comfortable when the weather was bad. His father, who was a lawyer, had wanted him to enter that profession, but Wilbur had been so sure of his own mind, and was so persistent that at his request he had been permitted to go to the Colorado Ranger School. From this he had returned even more enthusiastic than before, and Masseth, seeing that by temperament Wilbur was especially fitted for the Forest Service, had urged the boy's father to allow him to enter for it, and did not attempt to conceal his satisfaction with Wilbur's success.

"Why, Masseth, how did you get hold of Loyle?" asked the Chief Forester as the two came up the walk together.

"Didn't you know he was my nephew?" was the surprised reply.

"No," answered their host as they paused on the threshold, "he never said anything to me about it."

The geologist looked inquiringly at his young relative.

"I thought," said Wilbur, coloring, "that if I said anything about knowing you, before I was appointed, it would look as though I had done it to get a pull. I didn't think it would do me any good, anyhow; and even if it had, I felt that I'd rather not get anything that way."

"It wouldn't have helped you a bit," said the Chief Forester, "and, as you see, you did not need it. I'm glad, too, that you did not mention it at the time." He nodded his appreciation of the boy's position as they passed into the room beyond.

The place was thoroughly typical of the gathering and the occasion. The walls were hung with some magnificent trophies, elk and moose heads, one stuffed fish of huge size was framed beside the door, and there were numberless photographs of trees and forests, cross-sections of woods, and comparisons of leaves and seeds. Although in the heart of Washington, there was a breath and fragrance in the room, which, to the boy, seemed like old times in the woods. The men, too, that were gathered there showed themselves to be what they were—men who knew the great wide world and loved it. Every man seemed hearty in manner and thoroughly interested in whatever was going on.

Masseth was called away, soon after they entered the room, and Wilbur, left to himself, sauntered about among the groups of talkers, looking at the various trophies hung on the walls. As he drew near to one of the smaller groups, however, he caught the word "gun-play," so he edged up to the men and listened. One of them, seeing the lad, moved slightly to one side as an unspoken invitation to be one of them, and Wilbur stepped up.

The man who was speaking was comparing the present peaceful administration of the forests with the conditions that used to exist years ago, before the Service had been established, and when the Western "bad man" was at the summit of his power.

17

"It was during the cattle and sheep war that a fellow had to be pretty quick on the draw," said one.

"The Service had a good enough man for that, all right," suggested another member of the same group, "there wasn't any of them who could pull a bead quicker than our grazing Chief yonder." Wilbur turned and saw crossing the room a quiet-looking, spare man, light-complexioned, and apparently entirely inoffensive. "I guess they were ready enough to give him a wide berth when it came to gun-play."

"Talking about the cattle war," said the first speaker, "the worst trouble I ever had, or rather, the one that I hated to go into most, was back in those days. I was on the old Plum Creek Timber Land Reserve, now a portion of the Pike National Forest. A timber trespass sometimes leads to a very pretty scrap, and a cattle mix-up usually spells 'War' with a capital 'W,' but this had both."

"You get them that way sometimes," said a middle-aged, red-headed man, who was standing by.

"Had some down your way, too, I reckon?"

"Plenty of 'em. But go ahead with the yarn."

"Well, this bunch that I'm speaking of had skipped out from Montana; they were 'wanted' there, and they had come down and started cutting railroad ties in a secluded canyon forming one of the branches of West Plum Creek. They were hated good and plenty, these same tie-cutters, because they had a reputation of being too handy with their guns, and consequently causing a decrease in the calf crop. The cattlemen used to drop in on them every once in a while, but the tie-cutters were foxy, and they were never caught with the goods. Of course, there was a moral certainty that they weren't buying meat, but nothing could be proved against them, and the interchanges of compliments, while lively and picturesque enough, never took the form of lead, although it was expected every time they met."

"Had this been going on long?"

"Several months, I reckon," answered the former Ranger, "before I heard of it. This was just before that section of the country was taken over by the

Forest Service. As soon as notice was given that the district in question was to be placed under government regulations, a deputation to the tie-cutters loped down on their cow-ponies to convey the cheerful news. Expressing, of course, the profoundest sympathy for them, the spokesman of the cattle group volunteered the information that they could wrap up their axes in tissue paper, tie pink ribbons on their rifles and go home, because any one caught cutting timber on the reserve, now that it was a reserve, would go to the Pen for fifteen years."

"What a bluff!"

"Bluff it certainly was. It didn't work, either. One of the tie-cutters in reply suggested that the cowmen should go back and devote their time to buying Navajo saddle-blankets and silver-mounted sombreros, since ornamenting the landscape was all they had to do in life; another replied that if a government inspector ever set eyes on their cattle he'd drive them off the range as a disgrace to the State; and a third capped the replies with the terse answer that no ten United States officers and no hundred and ten cattlemen could take them out alive."

"That wouldn't make the cow-camp feel happy a whole lot," remarked the red-headed man.

"There wasn't any shooting, though, as I said before, though just how it kept off I never rightly could understand. At all events they fixed it so that we heard of it in a hurry. Then both sides awaited developments. The tie-cutters kept their hands off the cattle for a while, and the cowmen had no special business with railroad ties, so that, aside from snorting at each other, no special harm was done.

"But, of course, the timber trespass question had to be investigated, and the Supervisor, who was then located at Colorado Springs, arranged to make the trip with me to the tie-cutters' camp from a small station about fifty miles north of the Springs. I met him at the station as prearranged. We were just about to start when a telegram was handed him calling him to another part of the forest in a hurry."

"Tough luck," said one of the listeners.

"It surely was—for me," commented the narrator. "The camp to which we had intended going was twenty-six miles into the mountains, and going up there alone didn't appeal to me a little bit. However, the Supervisor told me to start right out, to get an idea of how much timber had been cut, and in what kind of shape the ground had been left, and in short, to 'nose around a little,' as he put it himself."

"That was hardly playing the game, sending you up there alone," said one of the men.

"I thought at the time that it wasn't, but what could he do? The matter had to be investigated, and he had been sent for and couldn't come with me. But he was considerate enough, strongly urging me not to get killed, 'as Rangers were scarce.'"

"That was considerate!"

"Yes, wasn't it? But early the next morning I started for the canyon where the outlaws were said to be in hiding. The riding was fair, so I made good time on the trail and got to the entrance of the canyon about the middle of the day. A few hundred feet from the fork of the stream I came to a little log cabin, occupied by a miner and his family. I took lunch with them and told them my errand. Both the man and his wife begged me not to go up to the camp alone, as they had heard the tie-cutters threaten to kill at sight any stranger found on their land."

"Why didn't you propose that the miner should go up to the camp with you?"

"I did. But he remarked that up to date he had succeeded in keeping out of the cattlemen-lumbermen trouble, and that he was going to keep right along keeping out. He suggested that if there was going to be any funeral in the immediate vicinity he wasn't hankering to take any more prominent part than that of a mourner, and that the title-rôle of such a performance wasn't any matter of envy with him. However, I succeeded in persuading him to come part of the way with me, and secured his promise that he would listen for any shooting, and if I should happen to resign involuntarily from the Service by the argument of a bullet, that he would volunteer as a witness in the case."

"I don't altogether blame him, you know," said the red-headed man; "you said he had a wife there, and interfering with other folks' doings isn't healthy."

"I didn't blame him either," said the first speaker, "but I would have liked to have him along. A little farther up the canyon I came to a recently built log cabin, covered with earth. An old man stood at the door and I greeted him cheerily. We had a moment's chat, and then I asked him the way to the cabin where the tie-cutters lived. Judge of my surprise when he told me this was their cabin, and that they lived with him. By the time I had secured this much information the two younger men had come out, and one of them, Tom, wanted to know what I was after. I stated my business, briefly. There was a pause.

"'Ye 'low as ye're agoin' to jedge them ties,' he said slowly. 'Wa'al I 'low we'll sort 'er go along. Thar's a heap o' fow-el in these yar parts, stranger, an' I 'low I'll take a gun.'

"The other brother, who seemed more taciturn, turned and nodded to two youngsters who had come out of the cabin while Tom was speaking. The elder of the two, a boy about thirteen years old, went into the shack and returned in a moment bringing out two rifles. I turned the broncho's head up the trail, but Tom interposed.

"'I 'low,' he said, 'that ye'll hev ter leave yer horse-critter right hyar; thar ain't much of er trail up the mount'n.'

"I wasn't particularly anxious to get separated from my horse, and that cabin was just about the last place I would have chosen to leave him; but there was no help for it, and as I would have to dismount anyway to get into the timber, I slipped out of the saddle and put the hobbles on. But when we came to start, the two men wanted me to go first. I balked at that. I told them that I wasn't in the habit of walking up a mountain trail in front of two men with guns, and that they would have to go first and show the

21

way. They grumbled, but, seeing that I meant it, they turned and silently walked up the mountainside ahead of me.

"They stopped at an old prospect shaft that was filled to the brim with water, and wanted me to come close to the hole and look at it, telling me some cock-and-bull story about it, and calling my attention to some supposed outcrop of rich ore that could be seen under the water. But I refused flatly to go a step nearer than I then was, telling them that I wished to get to those ties immediately.

"At an old cabin they halted again, and Tom wanted to know which was 'the best shot in the bunch.' I was not in favor of trying guns or anything of that sort, especially when there seemed no reason for it, knowing how easy it would be for a shot to go wide, and so I urged them to lead on to the ties. But Tom insisted upon shooting, and though his brother did not seem quite to follow the other's plans, still he chimed in with him, and the only thing I could do was to agree with what grace I could. But I decided to make this a pretext for disposing of some of their superfluous ammunition.

"Pulling my six-shooter, I told Jim to put an old sardine can, that was lying on the ground near by, on the stump of a tree about twenty-five or thirty yards distant. Then I told him to lean his rifle against the cabin while placing the can on the tree. This he did. I stepped over to the cabin and took the gun as though to look after it. Then I walked over to where Tom stood, telling him to blaze away at the can on the tree. While he was doing so I slipped the cartridges out of Jim's gun and put them in my pocket.

"By the time that Tom had fired three shots Jim came up and I told the former to hand over the rifle and let his brother try. Quite readily he did so. Of course, there were only two cartridges left in the gun, for it was a half-magazine, but Jim expected to take the third shot with his own rifle. When he had fired twice, however, and reached out his hand for the other gun, I handed it to him with the remark that it was empty. For a minute or two things looked black, because both men saw that they had been tricked. But I had the drop on them, and since they were both disarmed I felt considerably easier."

"How did it end up?" asked the red-haired listener.

"It was easy enough after that, as long as I didn't turn my back to them or let either get too near. We went together and counted the ties, returning to the cabin where I had left my horse. When the tie-cutters found, however, that the cattlemen had deliberately exaggerated the penalty for timber trespass in the hope that they would resist and thus get themselves into serious trouble with the government, their anger was diverted from me. By joining in with them in a sweeping denunciation of the cow-camp, and by pointing out that no harsh measures were intended against them, they came to look on me as friend instead of foe."

"What was done about the trespass?"

"It was pretty early in the days of the Service, and, as you remember, we let them down easily at first so that no undue amount of friction should be caused. I think some small fine, purely nominal, was exacted, and the tie-cutters got into harmonious relations with the Supervisor later. But those same boys told me, just as I was starting for home, that they intended to drop me in that old prospect shaft, or, failing that, to pump me full of holes."

The speaker had hardly finished when a scattering of groups and an unfolding of chairs took place and the lecturer for the evening was announced. He won Wilbur's heart at once by an appreciative story of a young Chinese boy, a civil service student in his native province, who had accompanied him on a portion of his trip through China in order to learn what might be done toward the improvement of his country.

"He was a bright lad, this Fo-Ho," said the lecturer, "and it was very largely owing to him that I extended my trip a little and went to Fou-Ping. I visited Fo-Ho's family home, where the graves of his ancestors were—you know how powerful ancestor-worship still is in China. Such a scene of desolation I never saw, and, I tell you, I was sorry for the boy. There was the town that had been his father's home deserted and in ruins.

"Two hundred years before, in this same place now so thickly strewn with ruins, there had been no one living, and the mountains were accounted impassable because of the dense forests. But in 1708 a Mongol horde under a powerful chieftain settled in the valley, and the timber began to be cut recklessly. Attracted by the fame of this chieftain, other tribes poured down into these valleys, until by 1720 several hundred thousand persons were living where thirty years before not a soul was to be seen. The cold winters of Mongolia drew heavily upon the fuel resources of the adjacent forests, and a disastrous fire stripped hundreds of square miles. Farther and farther afield the inhabitants had to go for fuel, until every stick which would burn had been swept clear; bleaker and more barren grew the vicinity, until at last the tribes had to decamp, and what was once a dense forest and next a smiling valley has become a hideous desert which even the vultures have forsaken."

Masseth leaned over toward Wilbur and whispered:

"You don't have to go as far away as China. There are some terrible cases of deforestation right here in the United States."

The lecturer then launched into a description of the once great forests of China, and quoted the words of writers less than three centuries ago who depicted the great Buddhist monasteries hid deep in the heart of densely wooded regions. Then, with this realization of heavily forested areas in mind, there was flashed upon the screen picture after picture of desolation. Cities, once prosperous, were shown abandoned because the mountains near by had become deforested. Man could not live there because food could not grow without soil, and all the soil had been washed away from the slopes. The streams, once navigable, were choked up with the silt that had washed down. When rains came they acted as torrents, since there was no vegetation to hold the water and the lower levels became flooded.

"Nature made the world a garden," said the speaker, "and man is making it a desert. Our children and our children's children for countless generations are to enjoy the gardens we leave, or bewail the deserts we create."

Startling, too, was the manner in which the lecturer showed the unhappy fate of countries which an unthinking civilization had despoiled. The hills and valleys where grew the famous cedars of Lebanon are almost treeless now, and Palestine, once so luxuriant, is bare and lonely. Great cities flourished upon the banks of the Tigris and Euphrates where were the hanging gardens of Babylon and the great hunting parks of Nineveh, yet now the river runs silently between muddy banks, infertile and deserted, save for a passing nomad tribe. The woods of ancient Greece are not less ruined than her temples; the forests of Dalmatia whence came the timber that built the navies of the ancient world are now barren plateaus, shelterless and waste; and throughout a large part of southern Europe and northern Africa, man has transformed the smile of nature into a mask of inflexible severity.

"But," said Wilbur, turning excitedly to his uncle, as soon as the lecturer had closed, "isn't there anything that can be done to make those places what they were before?"

"Not often, if it is allowed to go too far," said the geologist. "It takes time, of course, for all the soil to be washed away. But wherever the naked rock is exposed the case is hopeless. You can't grow anything, even cactus, on a rock. Lichens, of course, may begin, but hundreds of thousands of years are required to make soil anew."

"But if it's taken in time?"

"Then you can reforest by planting. But that's slow and costly. It requires millions of dollars to replant a stretch of forest which would have renewed itself just by a little careful lumbering, for Nature is only too ready to do the work for nothing if given a fair chance."

By this time the gathering had broken up in large part and a number of those who had come only to hear the lecture had gone. Some of the Forest Service men, however, were passing through the corridors to the dining-room. At the door Wilbur paused hesitatingly. He had not been invited to stay, but at the same time he felt that he could hardly leave without thanking his uncle, who at the time was strolling toward the other portion of the house, deeply engrossed in conversation. In this quandary the Chief Forester, all unknown to the lad, saw his embarrassment, and with the quick intuition so characteristic of the man, divined the cause.

"Come along, Loyle, come along in," he said, "you're one of us now."

Wilbur, with a grateful look, passed on into the reception-room. A moment later he heard his name called, and, turning, came face to face with a tall young fellow, bronzed and decisive looking.

"My name's Nally," he said, "and I hear you're going to one of my forests. Mr. Masseth was telling me that you're his nephew. I guess we'll start right in by having our first feed together. This is hardly camping out," he added, looking around the well-appointed and handsome room, "but the grub shows that it's the Service all right."

The District Forester motioned to the table which was heaped with dozens upon dozens of baked apples, flanked by several tall pitchers of milk.

"There you have it," he continued, "back to nature and the simple life. It's all right to go through a Ranger School and to satisfy the powers that be about your fitness, but that isn't really getting to the inside of the matter. It's when you feel that you've had the chance to come right in and take the regular prescribed ritual of a baked apple and a glass of milk in the house of the Chief Forester that you can feel you're the real thing in the Service."

CHAPTER III
THE FIGHT IN THE COULEE

When, a few days later, Wilbur found himself standing on the platform of the little station at Sumber, with the cactus-clad Mohave desert about him and the slopes of the Sierra Nevada beyond, he first truly realized that his new life was beginning. His journey out from Washington had been full of interest because the District Forester had accompanied him the greater part of the way, and had taken the opportunity to explain how varied were the conditions that he would find in the Sequoia forest to which he had been assigned. In large measure the District Forester's especial interest, Wilbur realized, was due to the fact that Masseth had told him of the boy's intention to go to college and thence through the Yale Forestry School, having had beforehand training as Guard, and possibly later as Ranger.

But, as the train pulled out of the station, and Wilbur looked over the sage-brush and sparse grass, seeming to dance under the shimmering heat-waves of the afternoon sun, he suddenly became conscious that the world seemed very large and that everything he knew was very far away. The strange sense of doubt as to whether he were really himself, a curious feeling that the desert often induces, swept over him, and he was only too ready to enter into conversation when a small, wiry man, with black hair and quick, alert eyes, came up to him with the rolling walk that betokens a life spent in the saddle, and said easily:

"Howdy, pard!"

The boy returned a friendly "Good-afternoon," and waited for the stranger to continue.

"She looks some as if you was the whole pack on this deal," was the next remark.

"Well," replied Wilbur, looking at him quizzically, "I wasn't conscious of being crowded here."

The range-rider followed the boy's glance around the immediate neighborhood, noting the station agent and the two or three figures in front of the general store, who formed the sum of the visible population, and nodded.

"Bein' the star performer, then," he went on, "it might be a safe bet that you was sort of prospectin' for the Double Bar J."

"That was the name of the ranch," said the boy. "I was told to go there and get a couple of ponies."

"An' how was you figurin' on gettin' to the ranch? Walkin'?"

"Not if I could help it. And that," he added, pointing to the desert, "I should think would be mean stuff to walk on."

"Mean she is," commented Wilbur's new acquaintance, "but even s'posin' that you did scare up a pony, how did you dope it out that you would hit up the right trail? This here country is plumb tricky. And the trail sort of takes a nap every once in a while and forgets to show up."

"I didn't expect to find my way alone," said the boy. "If nobody had been here, I'd have found somebody to show me —"

"Hold hard," said the cowboy, interrupting, "till I look over that layout. If you hadn't ha' found anybody, you'd ha' found somebody? Shuffle 'em up a bit, pard, and try a new deal."

"But," continued Wilbur, not paying any attention to the interruption, "I fully expected that some one from the ranch would be here to meet me."

"If all your conjectoors comes as near bein' accurate as that same," said the other, "you c'd set up as a prophet and never call the turn wrong. Which I'm some attached to the ranch myself."

"I thought you were, probably," said Wilbur, "and I'm much obliged to you, if you came to meet me."

"That's all right! But if you're ready, maybe we'd better start interviewin' the scenery on the trail. How about chuck?"

"Thanks," said the boy, "I had dinner on the car."

"An' you're thirsty none?"

"Not especially. But," he added, not wishing to offend his companion, "if you are, go ahead."

"Well, if you don't mind," began the other, then he checked himself. "I guess I c'n keep from dyin' of a cracked throat until we get there," he added. "C'n you ride?"

"Yes!" said Wilbur decisively.

The cowboy turned half round to look at him with a dubious smile.

"You surely answers that a heap sudden," he said. "An' I opine that's some risky as a general play."

"Why?" asked the boy.

"Bein' too sure in three-card Monte has been a most disappointin' experience to many a gent, an' has been most condoocive to transfers of ready cash."

"But that's just guessing," said Wilbur. "I'm talking of what I know."

"Like enough you never heard about Quick-Finger Joe?" queried the cowboy. "Over-confidence hastens his exit quite some."

"No," answered Wilbur quickly, scenting a story, "I never even heard of him. Who was he?"

"This same Joe," began the range-rider, "is a tow-haired specimen whose manly form decorates the streets of this here metropolis of Sumber that you've been admirin'. He has the name of bein' the most agile proposition on a trigger that ever shot the spots off a ten o' clubs. He makes good his reputation a couple of times, and then gets severely left alone. To him, one day, while he is standin' takin' a little refreshment, comes up a peaceful and inoffensive-lookin' stranger, who has drifted into town promiscuous-like in the course of the afternoon. He addresses Joe some like this:

"'Which I hears with profound admiration that you're some frolicsome and speedy on gun-play?'

"Joe, tryin' to hide his blushes, admits that his hand can amble for his hip right smart. Whereupon the amiable-appearin' gent makes some sort of comment, just what no one ever knew, but it seems tolerable superfluous an' sarcastic, an' instantaneous there's two shots. When the smoke clears away a little, Joe is observed to be occupyin' a horizontal position on the floor and showin' a pronounced indisposition to move. The stranger casually remarks:

"'Gents, this round's on me. I shore hates to disturb your peaceful converse on a balmy evenin' like this yere in a manner so abrupt an' sudden-like. But he had to get his, some time, an' somebody's meditations would hev to be disturbed. This hyar varmint, gents, what is now an unopposed candidate for a funeral pow-wow, was a little too previous with his gun agin my younger brother. It's a case of plain justice, gents; my brother was without weapons, and he—' pointing to the figure on the floor, 'he knew it. Line up, gents, and give it a name!'"

"What did they do to the stranger?" asked Wilbur eagerly, divided between admiration of the quickness of the action and consternation at the gravity of the result.

"They compliments him some on the celerity of his shootin', and feels a heap relieved by Joe's perpetual absence. An' the moral o' this little tale is that you're hittin' a fast clip for trouble when you go around prompt and aggressive to announce your own virtoos. I'm not advancin' any criticism as to your shinin' talents in the way of ridin', pard, but you haven't been long enough in this here vale of tears to be what you might call experienced."

"I've ridden a whole lot," said Wilbur, who was touchy on the point and proud of his horsemanship, "and while I don't say that there isn't a horse I can't ride, I can say that I've never seen one yet. I started in to ride pretty nearly as soon as I started to walk."

"I don't want to mar your confidence none," replied the cowboy, "an' I likes a game sport who'll bet his hand to the limit, though I generally drops my stake on the other side. But if some mornin' you sh'd find the ground rearin' up and hittin' you mighty sudden, don't forget that I gave you a plain steer. Here's your cayuse."

Wilbur had been a little disappointed that the cowboy should not have shown up as ornamentally as he had expected, not wearing goatskin "chaps" or rattlesnake hatbands, and not even having a gorgeous saddle-blanket on his pony, but the boy felt partly rewarded when he saw him just put his toe in the stirrup and seem to float into the saddle. The pony commenced dancing about in the most erratic way, but Wilbur noted that his companion seemed entirely unaware that the horse was not standing still, although his antics would have unseated any rider that the boy previously had seen. He was conscious, moreover, that his climb into his own saddle was very different from that which he had witnessed, but he really was a good rider for a boy, and felt quite at home as soon as they broke into the loping canter of the cow-pony.

"I understood," said Wilbur as they rode along, "that I should meet the Ranger at the ranch. His name was given to me as Rifle-Eye Bill, because I was told he had been a famous hunter before he joined the Service. I thought at first you might be the Ranger, but he was described to me as being very tall."

"Which he does look some like a Sahaura cactus on the Arizona deserts," said the range-rider, "an' I surely favor him none. But that mistake of yours naterally brings it to me that I haven't what you might say introdooced myself. Which my baptismal handle is more interestin' than useful, an' I lays it by. So I'll just hand you the title under which I usually trots, bein' 'Bob-Cat Bob,' ridin' for the Double Bar J."

"Not having risen to any later title," said Wilbur good-humoredly, "I've got to be satisfied with the one I started with. I'm generally called Wilbur."

"Which is sure unfamiliar to me. I opine it's a new brand on the range." He flourished his sombrero in salute, so that his pony bucked twice and then tried to bolt. Wilbur watched and envied him the absolute ease with which he brought down the broncho to a quiet lope again.

"I'm going to join the Forest Service," the boy explained, knowing that according to the etiquette of the West no question would be asked about his business, but that he would be expected to volunteer some statement, "and my idea in coming to the ranch was to pick up a couple of horses and go on to the forest with the Ranger. I understand the Supervisor, Mr. Merritt, is very busy with some timber sales, and I didn't know whether the Ranger would be able to get away."

"I kind o' thought you might be headed for the Forest Service, since you was goin' along with Rifle-Eye," said the cowboy. "An' if you're goin' with him, you'll be all right."

"The Service looks pretty good to me," said Wilbur.

"I've no kick comin' agin the National Forests," said Bob-Cat, "we've always been treated white enough. Of course, there's always some soreheads who want to stampede the range and gets peevish when they're balked, but I guess the Service is a good thing all round. It don't appeal none to me, o' course. If I held all the cards, I'd rip down every piece of barbed wire west of the Mississippi, let the sheepmen go to the ranges beside the canals o' Mars or some other ekally distant region, an' git back to the good old days o' the Jones 'n' Plummer trail. But then, I sure enough realize that I'm not the only strikin' feature o' the landscape an' there's others that might have a say."

"I guess the present way is the best in the long run at that, for all I hear," said Wilbur, "because every one now has a fair show. You can't have cattle and sheep overrunning everywhere without absolutely ruining the forests. Especially sheep. They can destroy a forest and make it as though it had never existed."

"I'm huggin' love of sheep none," said the cowboy, "an' my mental picter of the lower regions is a place what smells strong of sheep. But I sure miss my throw on any idee as to how they could do up a forest of big trees."

"They do, just the same."

"How? Open her up, pard, an' explain. I'm listenin' mighty attentive."

"This way," began the boy, remembering some of the talks he had heard at the Ranger School. "When a dry year comes, if the sheep are allowed into the forest, the grass, which is poor because of the dryness, soon gets eaten down. Then the sheep begin to browse on the young shoots and seedlings, and even will eat the leaves off the young saplings that they can reach, thus destroying all the baby trees and checking the growth of those that are a little more advanced. When this goes on for two or three seasons all the young growth is gone. Since there are no saplings, no young shoots, and no seedlings, the forest never recovers, but becomes more like a park with stretches of grass between clumps of trees. Then, when these trees die, there are no others to take their place and the forest is at an end."

"How about cattle?"

"They're not nearly as bad. Cattle won't eat leaves unless they have to. And they don't browse so close, nor pack down the ground as hard with their hoofs. If there's grass enough to go round, cattle won't injure a forest much, but, of course, the grazing has got to be restricted or else the same sort of thing will happen that goes on when sheep are let in."

"Never knew before," said the boy's companion, "why I ought ter hate sheep. Jest naterally they're pizen to me, but I never rightly figured out why I allers threw them in the discard. Now I know. There's a heap of satisfaction in that. It's like findin' that a man you sure disagreed with in an argyment is a thunderin' sight more useful to the community dead than he was alive. It don't alter your feelin's none, but it helps out strong on the ensooin' explanations."

"Are there many sheep out here?"

"There's a tidy few. But it's nothin' like Montana. You ought ter get Rifle-Eye Bill to tell you of the old days o' the sheep an' cattle war. The debates were considerable fervent an' plenty frequent, an' a Winchester or two made it seem emphatic a whole lot."

"Was Rifle-Eye mixed up in it?"

"Which he's allers been a sort of Florence Nightingale of the Rockies, has old Rifle-Eye," was the reply. "I don't mean in looks — but if a feller's shot up or hurt, or anythin' of that kind, it isn't long before the old hunter turns up, takes him to some shack near by and persuades somebody to look after him till he gets around again. An' we've got a little lady that rides a white mare in these here Sierras who's a sure enough angel. I don't want to know her pedigree, but when it comes to angels, she's It. An' when she an' Rifle-

Eye hitches up to do the ministerin' act, you'd better believe the job's done right. I never heard but of one man that ever said 'No' to Rifle-Eye, no matter what fool thing he asked."

"How was that?" asked Wilbur.

"It was the wind-up of one o' these here little differences of opinion on the sheep question, same as I've been tellin' you of. It happened somewhar up in Oregon, although I've forgotten the name o' the ranch. Rifle-Eye could tell you the story better'n I can, but he won't. It was somethin' like this:

"There was a big coulee among the hills, an', one summer, when there'd been a prairie fire that wiped out a lot o' feed, a bunch o' cattle was headed into this coulee. Three cowpunchers and a cook with the chuck wagon made up the gang. But this yar cook was one o' them fellers what's not only been roped by bad luck, but hog-tied and branded good and plenty. He had been the boss of a ranch, a small one, but he'd fallen foul o' the business end of a blizzard, an' he'd lost every blamed head o' cattle that he had. He lost his wife, too."

"How did she come in on it?"

"It was this way. She heard, or thought she heard, some one callin' outside, a little ways from the house. She s'posed, o' course, that it was the men who had tackled the storm in the hope o' savin' some o' the cattle, an' she ran out o' the door to give 'em an answerin' hail so as they could git an idee as to the direction o' the house. But she hadn't gone but a few steps when the wind caught her—leastways, that was how they figured it out afterwards—and blew her along a hundred feet or so before she could catch breath, and then she stumbled and fell. She got up, sort o' dazed, most like, and tried to run back to the shack. But in the blindin' snow nothin' o' the house could be seen, an' though she tried to fight up in that direction against the wind, she must have gone past it a little distance to the left. They didn't find her until two days after when the blizzard had blown itself out, an' there she was, stone dead, not more than a half a mile away from the house.

"The boss was near crazy when they found her, an' he never was fit for much afterwards. There was a child, only a little shaver then, who was asleep in the house at the time his mother run out to answer the shout she reckoned she heard. So, since the rancher wasn't anyways overstocked on female relations, an' he had the kid to look after, the one-time boss went out as a camp cook an' took the boy along. He was rustlin' the chuck for this bunch I'm a-tellin' you about, that goes into the coulee.

"By 'n' by, a week or so afterward, a herd o' sheep comes driftin' into this same valley, bein' ekally short for feed, an' the herders knocks up a sort o' corral an' looks to settle down. The cowpunchers pays 'em an afternoon call, an' suggests that the air outside the coulee is a lot healthier for sheep—an' sheepmen—an' that onless they makes up their minds to depart, an' to make that departure a record-breaker for speed, they'll make their relatives sure a heap mournful. The sheepmen replies in a vein noways calculated to bring the dove o' peace hoverin' around, an' volunteers as a friendly suggestion that the cattlemen had best send to town and order four nice new tombstones before ringin' the curtain up on any gladiatorial pow-wow. When the cowpunchers rides back, honors is even, an' each side is one man short.

"Now, this coulee, which is the scene of these here operations, is so located that there's only one way out. Most things in life there's more, but in this here particular coulee, the openin' plays a lone hand. As the cattlemen got there first, and went 'way back to the end o' the ravine, the sheepmen are nearer to what you might call the valley door. If the cowpunchers could have made a get-away, it's a cinch that they'd have headed for the ranch an' brought back enough men with them to make their persuasion plenty urgent. But the herders ain't takin' any chances of allowin' the other side to better their hand, an' when, one night, a cowpuncher tries to rush it, they pots him as pretty as you please. The cook, who's cuddlin' his Winchester at the time, fires at the flash and disposes o' the herder, sort o' evenin' matters up. This leaves only one cowpuncher and the cook. There's still three men at the herders' camp.

"Then the cook, he indooces a bullet to become sufficient intimate with one o' the herder's anatomy, but gits a hole in the leg himself an' is laid up. The other cowpuncher runs the gauntlet an' gits out safe. He hikes back the next day with a bunch o' boys, an' they follows up the herders an' wipes out that camp for fair, an' stampedes the herd over the nearest canyon. Then they circles back to the coulee to pick up the cook.

"When they gits there, they surely finds themselves up against evidences of a tragedy. The cook, he's lyin' on the floor of the shack, dead as a nail, an' near him is the kid, who's still holdin' a table-knife in his hand, but who's lyin' unconscious from a wound in the head. The way they dopes it out, there's been a free-for-all fight in the place between the two remainin' herders an' the wounded cook, an' it looks some as if the kid had tried to help his dad by jabbin' at the legs o' the herders with a knife and been booted in the side o' the head to keep him quiet."

"How old was the youngster, then, Bob-Cat?" asked Wilbur.

"Seven or eight, I guess, maybe not so much," replied the other, "a nice, bright little kid, so I've heard. But there was somethin' broke, I reckon, by the blow he had, an' he never got over it. The boys took him back to the ranch an' doctored him the best they knew how, but they was buckin' fate an' had to quit, lettin' the kid git better or worse as it might turn out."

"But where does Rifle-Eye come in?"

"This way. Just before round-up, Rifle-Eye comes along, showin' he has the whole story salted down, though where he larned it gits me, and proposes that sence it was the sheepmen that injured the lad, it's up to them to look after him. At first the boys objects, sayin' that the kid was a cowpuncher's kid, but Rifle-Eye convinces 'em that the youngster's locoed for fair, that he's likely to stay that way for good an' all, and sence they agrees they can't ever make anythin' out of him, they lets him go.

"Then Rifle-Eye, he takes this unfortunate kid to the man that owned the sheep. He's a big owner, this man, and runs thirty or forty herds. The old hunter—this was all before he was a Ranger, you know—he puts it right up to the sheep-owner, who's a half-Indian, by the way, an' tells him that he's got to look after the boy. The old skinflint says 'No,' and this here, as I was sayin', is the only time that any one ever turned down old Rifle-Eye."

"And what happened to the boy?" queried Wilbur.

"The old hunter tries to shame this here sheep-owner into doin' the right thing, but he didn't have any more shame in him than a turkey buzzard; an' then he tries to bluff him an' says he'll make him keep the kid, but the old sinner jest whined around an' wouldn't give any sort o' satisfaction at all. So Rifle-Eye, he shakes the dust o' that house off'n his feet so good an' hard that he mighty nearly shakes the nails out of his boot-heels, an' hunts up a legal shark. Then an' there he adopts this half-witted youngster, an' has kep' him ever sence."

"How long ago was this?"

"Fifteen years an' more, I reckon. The kid's big now, an' strong as a bull moose, but he's a long way from bein' right in his head. He lives up in the woods, a piece back here, an' I reckon you'll find Rifle-Eye there as often as you will at his own cabin further along the range, although he never sleeps indoors at either place."

"Never sleeps indoors?"

"That's a straight string. He's got a decent enough shack where the boy is, but as soon as it gits dark, old Rifle-Eye he jest makes a pile o' cedar boughs, builds up a fire, an' goes to sleep. For fifty years he ain't slept under a roof summer or winter, an' when once he was in a town over-night, which was about the boy, as I was tellin' ye, he had to get up an' go on the roof to sleep. Lucky," added Bob-Cat with a grin, "it was a flat roof."

"Fifty years is a long time," commented the boy.

"Old Rifle-Eye ain't any spring chicken. He shouldered a musket in the Civil War, an' durin' the Indian mix-ups was generally found floatin' around wherever the fun was thickest. He was mighty close friends with the Pacific scout, old 'Death-on-th'-Trail,' who handed in his time at Portland not long ago."

"Handed in his time?" questioned Wilbur, then, as the meaning of the phrase flashed upon him, "oh, yes, I see, you mean he died."

"Sure, pard, died. You ought ter git Rifle-Eye Bill to spin you some yarns about 'Death-on-th'-Trail.' He'll deny that he's any shakes himself, but he'll talk about his old campmate forever."

The cowboy pointed with his hand to a long, low group of buildings that had just come within sight.

"See, Wilbur," he said, "there's the Double Bar J."

CHAPTER IV
PICKING A LIVELY BRONCHO

On seeing the ranch, Bob-Cat and Wilbur had put their ponies to a burst of speed and in a few minutes they reached the corral. The buildings, while comfortable enough, were far from pretentious, and even their strangeness scarcely made up to the boy for the lack of the picturesque. Then, of course, the fact that the cattle at that time of year were scattered all over the range and consequently that none of them were in sight, rendered it still less like his ideal of a cattle ranch, where he had half expected to see thousands of long-horned cattle tossing their heads the while that cowboys galloped around them shouting and firing off pistols.

In contrast with this, the dwelling, the bunk-house, the cooking shack, and the other frame sheds, all of the neutral gray that unpainted wood becomes when exposed to the weather, seemed very unexciting indeed. But when the lad turned to the corral, he felt that there was compensation there. Several hundred horses were in the enclosure, of many colors and breeds, but the greater part of them Indian ponies, or containing a strain of the mustang, and smaller and shaggier than the horses he had been accustomed to ride in his Illinois home.

The boy turned to his companion, his eyes shining with excitement.

"Do you suppose that I can buy any of those horses that I want to?" he said.

"If you're totin' along a pile of dinero, you might," was the reply, "but there's a few cayuses in there that would surely redooce a big roll o' bills to pretty skinny pickin's. For example, this little bay I'm ridin' now ain't any special wonder, an' maybe he's only worth about fifty dollars, but you can't buy him for five hundred. I reckon, though, you c'n trot away with most of 'em in there for ninety or a hundred dollars apiece."

"I hadn't expected to pay more than seventy or seventy-five," said Wilbur, his native shrewdness coming to the front, "and I think I ought to be able to pick up a good horse or two for that, don't you think?"

"There's allers somethin' that ain't worth much to be got cheap," said the cowboy, "but I don't look friendly none on payin' a cheap price for a horse.

Speakin' generally, there's somethin' that every feller likes a whole lot, an' out here, where domestic life ain't our chief play, it's mostly a horse. Leastways, when I hit the long trail, I'll be just as sorry to leave some ponies behind as I will humans."

"A horse can be a great chum," assented Wilbur. "So can a dog."

"No dogs in mine," said Bob-Cat emphatically, "they reminds me too much o' sheep. But when it comes to a horse, I tell ye, there's a lot more in the deal than buyin' an animal to carry you; there's buyin' somethin' that all the money in the world can't bring you sometimes — an' that's a friend."

Wilbur waited a moment without reply, and then the cowboy, deliberately changing the topic to cloak any strain of sentiment which he thought he might have been betrayed into showing, continued:

"How about saddles?"

"I'd been thinking about that," replied the boy, "and I thought I'd wait until I got out here before deciding. You can't use an English saddle-tree, of course, and I hate it anyway, and one like yours is too big. Those lumbering Mexican saddles always look to me as if they were as big a load for a little pony to carry as a man."

"Sure, they're heavy. But you can't do any ropin' without them. If you try 'n' rope on a small saddle the girth'll pretty near cut a pony in two. But you ain't got any ropin' to do, so I sh'd think an army saddle-tree would be about right. There's Rifle-Eye Bill comin' out of the bunk-house now. Ask him. He'll know."

Wilbur looked up, and saw emerging from the door of the bunk-house a tall, gaunt mountaineer. He strolled over to the corral with a long, loose-jointed stride.

"Got him, all right, Bob-Cat, did you?" he said in a measured drawl, then, turning to the boy, added: "Glad to see you, son."

"I've been hearing all about you, sir," answered Wilbur, "and I'm awfully glad to meet you here." He was about to dismount, but noting that Bob-Cat had merely thrown a leg over the horn of his saddle, he stayed where he was.

The old Ranger looked him over critically and closely, so that Wilbur felt himself flushing under the direct gaze, though he met the clear gray eye of his new acquaintance without flinching. Presently the latter turned to the range-rider.

"What do you think of him?" he asked in a slow, curiously commanding way.

Bob-Cat squirmed uneasily.

"You is sure annoyin'," he said in an aggrieved manner, "askin' me to go on record so plumb sudden. I'm no mind-reader."

There was a pause, but the Ranger quietly waited.

"It's embarrassin'," said Bob-Cat, "to try an' trot out a verdic' on snap-jedgment. I don't know."

Rifle-Eye, quite unperturbed, looked at him steadily and inquiringly.

"You know what you think," he said.

"He's sure green," replied the cowboy, shrugging his shoulders in protest, "an' he ain't much more humble-minded than a hen that's jest laid an egg of unusooal size, but I reckon he's got the makin's."

"It's a good thing to be green," said the old Ranger thoughtfully, "nothin' grows much after it's dry, Bob-Cat. The heart's got to be green anyway. Ye git hard to bend an' easy to break when ye're gettin' old."

"Then it's a cinch you'll never get old," promptly responded the other.

But the mountaineer continued talking, half to himself:

"An' he's too sure of himself! Wa'al, he's young yet. I've seen a pile o' sickness in my day, Bob-Cat, but that's about the easiest one to cure there is."

"What is?"

"Bein' young. Well, son, ye'd better turn the pony in."

The boy dismounted, and, half in pique at the dubious character given him by Bob-Cat and half in thanks for the meeting at the station and the ride, he turned to the cowboy, and said:

"I'm glad I've 'got the makings' anyway, and I'm much obliged, Bob-Cat, for all the yarns you told me on the trail. But, next time I come to the ranch I'll try not to be as green, and I know I'll not be as young."

The cowboy laughed.

"It's no use tryin' to dodge Rifle-Eye," he said. "You stand about as good a chance as if you was tryin' to sidestep a blizzard or parryin' the charge from a Gatlin' gun. If he asks a question you can gamble every chip in your pile that you're elected, and you've got to ante up with the answer whether it suits your hand or no."

Wilbur, following the suggestion of the Ranger, unsaddled his pony, turned him into the corral, and hung his saddle on the fence. Then together they went up to the house, where Wilbur met the boss, and after a few moments' chat they returned to the corral.

As the lad had come to the ranch especially for the purpose of buying a couple of ponies, he was anxious to transact the business as quickly as possible, and together with Bob-Cat and Rifle-Eye he scanned the horses in the enclosure, endeavoring to display, as he did so, what little knowledge of horseflesh he possessed. After the boy had commented on several, Rifle-Eye pointed out first one and then a second which he had previously decided on as being the best animals for the boy. But Wilbur's eye was attracted to a fine sorrel, and, turning to Rifle-Eye, he said decidedly:

"I want that one!"

The old Ranger, remarking quietly that it was a fine horse, but not suitable to the purpose for which Wilbur wanted the animal, passed on to the discussion of several other ponies near by, teaching the boy to discern the fine points of a horse, not for beauty, but for service.

But as soon as he had finished speaking, after a purely perfunctory assent, Wilbur burst out again:

41

"But, Rifle-Eye, I really want that sorrel most."

"You really think you want him?"

"Yes!"

"You wouldn't if you knew a little more about horses, son," said the Ranger. "It's all right to be sure what you want, but what you want is to be sure that what you want is right."

"Oh, I'm sure I'm right," answered the boy confidently.

"You can't be too careful choosin' a horse," commented Rifle-Eye. "Choosin' a horse is a good deal like pickin' out a sugar pine for shakes. You know what shakes are?"

"No, Rifle-Eye," answered the boy.

"They're long, smooth, split sheets of wood that the old-timers used for shingles. There's lots of sugar pine that'll make the finest kind o' lumber, an' all of it's good for fuel, but there ain't one tree in a hundred that'll split naturally an' easily into shakes. An' there ain't more'n one man in a hundred as can tell when a tree will do. But when you do get one just right, it's worth any ten other trees. An' the pine that's good ain't because it's a pretty tree to look at, or an easy one to cut down, or because of any other reason than that the grain's right. Same way with a horse. It ain't for his looks, nor for his speed, nor because he's easy to ride, nor for his strength you want him, but because his grain's right."

"Well, I'm sure that sorrel looks just right."

"Do looks always tell?"

"Oh, I can always tell a horse by his looks," replied Wilbur boastfully. "Anyhow, I want him."

"Persistent?" chuckled Bob-Cat, who was standing by enjoying every word, "why, cockle-burs ain't nothin' to him."

"But, supposin'," the old scout began gently, "I told you that the sorrel was the worst you could have, not the best?"

"But he ain't," broke in Bob-Cat, who could not bear to hear a friend's pony harshly criticised, "that's one of Bluey's string, an' he allers had good horses."

"There—you hear," said Wilbur triumphantly.

"I said—for the boy, Bob-Cat," answered the old Ranger firmly.

"I—I suppose you would have good reasons," said Wilbur, answering the old scout's question, "but I want him just the same, and I don't see why I can't buy him, if he's for sale. It's my money!"

"Sure, it's your money. An' the sorrel's a good horse," said the cowboy, to whom the persistence of Wilbur was giving great delight.

The Ranger slowly turned his head in silent rebuke, but although Bob-Cat was conscious of it, he was enjoying the fun too much to stop.

"You know he couldn't ride the sorrel, Bob-Cat," said Rifle-Eye reproachfully.

"But I can ride him, I know," said Wilbur. "I'm a good rider, really I am. And he looks gentle, besides. He is gentle, isn't he, Bob-Cat?"

"He's playful enough," was the reply, "some like a kitten, an' he surely is plenty restless in his habits. But where he shines is nerves. Why, pard, he c'd make a parcel of females besieged by a mouse look as if they was posin' for a picter, they'd be so still by comparison. But he's gentle, all right."

"I wouldn't want to try it if he was vicious, Rifle-Eye," said the boy appealingly, "but I really can ride, and he looks like a good horse."

"Are you buyin' this horse for your own pleasure or the work o' the Service? You're goin' to do your ridin' on my range, an' I reckon you'll admit I have some say."

"But I can break him to the work of the Service. Do let me try him!" Wilbur's persistence appeared in every look and word. "I don't see why I can't try, anyway, and then if I can't do it, there's no harm done."

"Can you throw a rope?" queried the Ranger.

"No," returned the boy promptly. "I never learned. But I can try."

"If you can't rope, how do you expect to saddle him? These ain't farm horses that you c'n harness or saddle while they eat oats out of your hand." He turned to the cowboy. "Can the sorrel be saddled without ropin'?"

"Bluey does," was the reply, "but I don't know that he'll let me."

"Won't you saddle him for me, Bob-Cat? I know I can ride him if I have a fair show."

The range-rider turned to the old Ranger.

"How about it?" he said. "The kid'll hunt leather for a while and then eat grass. But there's nothin' mean in the sorrel, an' he won't get hurt."

"I'll ride him," said Wilbur stoutly.

"You might, at that," rejoined Bob-Cat. "He's a game little sport, Rifle-Eye," he added, turning to the tall figure beside him, "why not let him play his hand out? You can't be dead sure how the spots will fall. Sure, I've twice seen an Eastern maverick driftin' into a faro game, an' by fools' luck cleanin' up the bank."

"If a man's a fool who depends on luck, what kind of a fool is the man who depends on fools' luck? You ain't playin' a square deal, Bob-Cat, in supportin' the lad to go on askin' to do what ain't good for him. But seein' you force my hand, why, you'd better go ahead now."

"I didn't force your hand none," replied the other, "I was merely throwin' out a suggestion."

"If I refuse the boy somethin' another man says is all right, doesn't that make it look as ef it was meanness in me? An' he goin' to work with me, too! What's the use o' sayin' that you ain't forcin' my hand? Givin' advice, Bob-Cat, ain't any go-as-you-please proposition; it's got to be thought out. Feelin's don't allers point the right trail to jedgment, an', as often as not, the blazes lead the wrong way. You're all right in your own way, Bob-Cat, but you're shy on roots, and your idees gets a windfall every time an extra puff comes along. You're like the trees settlers forgets about when they cuts on the outside of a forest an' ruins the inside."

"How is that?" asked Wilbur, anxious to divert the stream of Rifle-Eye's criticism from the cowboy, who had got himself into trouble defending him. "I didn't know there was any difference between a tree on the outside of a forest and one on the inside."

"Wa'al, then, I guess you're due to learn right now. If there's a tree of any size, standin' out by itself on a mountain side, with plenty of leaves, an' a big wind comes along, you c'n see easy enough that she presents a heap of surface to the wind. An' when a mountain gale gets up and blows fer fair, there's a pressure of air on that tree amountin' to several tons."

"Tons?" queried Bob-Cat incredulously.

"Tons," answered the old Banger. "A tree needs to have some strength in order to hold up its end. There's three ways o' doin' it. One is by havin' a lot more give in the fibers, more elastic like, so that the tree'll bend in the wind an' not get snapped off; another is by puttin' out a lot o' roots an' shovin' 'em in deep an' at the same time havin' a trunk that's plenty stout; an' the third is the thickenin' o' the trunk, right near the ground, where the greatest part o' the strain comes. An' all the various kinds o' trees works this out in different ways. But nothin's ever wasted, an' — "

"Oh, I see now," broke in Wilbur. "You're going to say that the trees which don't grow on the outside of a forest don't have to waste vitality into these forms of resistance."

"That's right. A tree that grows in a ravine, where there is little chance of a high wind, an' where light is scarce an' hard to get, such a tree will have a shallow root system an' a spindlin' trunk, all the growth havin' gone to height, an' a tree in the center of a forest is often the same way. The wind can't git through the forest, an' so the trees don't need ter prop themselves against it."

"Talk about yer eddicated trees!" ejaculated the cowboy, "which colleges is a fool to them."

"It's true enough, Bob-Cat, just the same. But supposin' a belt on the outside o' the forest is cut down, then the inner trees, thus exposed, haven't any proper weapons to fight the wind, an' they go down."

45

"Doesn't it take a very high wind to blow down some of these big trees?" asked Wilbur.

"Some kinds it does," said the Ranger, "but there's others that go down pretty easy, lodge-pole pine, fer instance. But a tree doesn't have to be blown down to be ruined. Even if a branch is blown off—an' you know how often that happens—insects and fungi get into the wound of the tree and decay follows."

"But you can't persuade the wind none," objected Bob-Cat. "If she's goin' to blow, she's goin' to blow, an' that's all there is to it."

"No, it ain't any use arguin' with a fifty-mile breeze, that's sure. But you can keep the inside trees from bein' blown down by leavin' uncut the deep-rooted trees on the outside. If you wanted a good big bit of timber, an' could cut it from a tree on the outside o' the forest, you'd take it first because it was handiest, wouldn't you?"

"I sure would."

"Yet, you see, it would ha' been the worst thing you could do. An' as I started out to say, that's where you get in wrong doin' things without thinkin'. Just like this ridin' idee to-day. By urgin' on the lad's nateral desire you make it hard fer him an' fer me."

"All right, Rifle-Eye," said Bob-Cat good-humoredly, "you've got me. I reckon I passes up this hand entire." He nodded and began to stroll away.

But Wilbur called him back.

"Oh, Bob-Cat," he cried, "aren't you going to saddle him for me now?"

The cowboy turned and grinned.

"Which you'd make tar an' feathers look sick for stickin' to a thing." Then, reading a grudging assent from Rifle-Eye, he continued: "Yep, I'll go an' saddle," and sauntered into the corral.

In a few minutes he came back, leading the sorrel. He was saddled and Bob-Cat had shortened up the stirrups. Wilbur jumped forward eagerly, put his foot in the stirrup, and was up like a flash. The sorrel never moved. The boy shook the reins a little and clucked his tongue against his teeth without any apparent result. Then Wilbur dug his heels into the pony's ribs.

Things began to happen. The sorrel went straight up in the air with all four feet, coming down with the legs stiff, giving Wilbur a jar which set every nerve twitching as though he had got an electric shock. But he kept his seat. Then the sorrel began pacing forward softly with an occasional sudden buck, each of which nearly threw him off and at most of which he had to "hunt leather," or in other words, catch hold of the saddle with his hands. Still he kept his seat.

Finding that these simpler methods did not avail, the sorrel began a little more aggressive bucking, fore and aft, "sun-fishing" and "weaving," and once or twice rearing up so straight that Wilbur was afraid the sorrel would fall over backwards on him, and he had heard of riders being killed that way. But he stole a glance at Rifle-Eye, and, seeing that the old Ranger was looking on quite unperturbed, he realized that there was no great danger. And still he kept his seat.

But as the sorrel warmed up to his work the boy began to realize that he had not the faintest chance of being able to wear the pony down. It was now only a question of how long he could stick on. He knew he would be done if the sorrel started to roll, but as yet the beast had shown no inclination that way. But as the bucks grew quicker and more jerky, Wilbur began to wonder within himself whether he would prefer to pitch over the pony's head or slide off over his tail. Suddenly, with a bound, the pony went up in the air and gave a double wriggle as he came down and Wilbur found himself on the ground before he knew what had happened. The sorrel, who, as Bob-Cat had said, was a gentle beast, stood quietly by, and the boy always afterwards declared that he could hear the horse chuckle.

The boy got up abashed and red in the face, because several other ranchmen had come up and were enjoying his confusion, but he tried to put a good face on it, and said:

"That's a bucker for fair."

"No," responded Bob-Cat, "that isn't bucking," and he swung himself into the saddle.

The sorrel commenced plunging and rearing again, this time with greater vigor. But Bob-Cat, taking a little bag of tobacco and some cigarette papers out of his pocket, quietly poured out some of the tobacco on the paper, rolled it carefully, and then lighted it, keeping his seat on the bucking broncho quite easily the while. This done, he dismounted, turning to the boy as he did so.

"She's easy enough. There's lots o' the boys, like Bluey, fer example, who really can ride," he continued, "that 'd just split with laughin' at the idee o' me showin' off in the saddle. I c'n rope with the best o' them, but I'm no buster. And some o' these here critters you've got to ride. See that big roan in there?"

Wilbur followed the direction of his finger and nodded.

"They call her 'Squealin' Bess,' an' you couldn't pay me to get on her back. Bluey c'n ride her; he's done it twice; but you c'n bet your last blue chip that he doesn't do it fer fun."

Wilbur turned to the old Ranger who had been standing silently by through the performance.

"I'm much obliged, Rifle-Eye," he said, "but I'd like to buy that sorrel just the same and learn to ride him."

For the first time the old Ranger smiled.

"You're somethin' like a crab, Wilbur," he said, "that grabs a stick viciously with his claw an' won't let go even when he's hauled up out o' the water. You c'n buy the sorrel if you want to, but he won't be any use to you up in the forest. Broncho-bustin' is an amusement you c'n keep for your leisure hours. But I'm thinkin', son, from what I know of the work you'll have to do, that you'll mostly be tired enough after a day's work to want to rest a while. But if you're sot, I s'pose you're sot. An' I'm old enough to know that it's no use hammerin' a mule when he's got his forelegs spread. Get whatever horses you like, I've got a saddle for you up at the bunk-house, an' you c'n meet me beyond the corral sunup to-morrow mornin'."

He nodded to the boys and turned on his heel, walking off in the direction of the river. Seeing that the fun was over the boys scattered, and Wilbur, finding that his friend Bob-Cat was going to stay at the ranch over-night, attached himself to him. But as soon as supper was over, the lad, finding himself stiffer than he had expected from his battle with the sorrel, partly because he had not been riding constantly for a couple of years, was glad to go to his bunk, listening to the breezy Western talk of the men and the yarns of cattle and of horses that they had to tell. He hardly knew that he had fallen asleep when Bob-Cat shook him, saying:

"Better tumble up, bub. Rifle-Eye is sure an early bird. He's some chanticleer, believe me. He's plumb convinced that if he ain't awake and up to greet the sun, it won't rise."

Wilbur laughed and "tumbled up" accordingly.

At breakfast, over the plentiful food served on tin plates and in tin mugs, Rifle-Eye was entirely silent, uttering never a word and paying no attention to any allusion about horses. Right after the meal Wilbur went down to the corral, saddled one of his two new horses, put a leading bridle on the other, and, after bidding Bob-Cat and the boys "Good-by," started for the point where he was to meet the Ranger.

As he rode up, the old frontiersman scanned carefully the two horses the boy had with him and his face cleared.

"What horses are those?" he asked.

"Oh, just a couple I got for the forest work," answered Wilbur with overdone carelessness.

They rode on in silence a few rods, then the old Ranger spoke again.

"Don't ever be afraid o' lettin' on you've made a mistake, son," he said; "the more mistakes you make the more you'll know. There's only one thing to remember, don't make the same mistake twice."

"I'll try not," said the boy.

The Ranger reined up beside the lad, and, reaching out his long, gaunt hand, patted the neck of the pony on which Wilbur was riding.

"They're half-sisters, those two," he said. "I raised 'em from colts myself. I rode the mother over these very trails, many and many's the time. This one is called Kit, after her."

Wilbur flushed at the remembrance of the manner in which before he had slighted the old scout's choice.

"Oh, Rifle-Eye," he said penitently, "if I'd only known!"

"You'll prize them more now," the Ranger said.

CHAPTER V

A TUSSLE WITH A WILD-CAT

"Bob-Cat was telling me," said Wilbur, as with the Ranger he rode through the arid and silvered grayness of the Mohave desert and reached the foothill country, "that before you entered the Service you were pretty well known as a hunter."

"Wa'al, son," the mountaineer replied, "I reckon I've done some kind o' huntin' for fifty years on end. But there's not much huntin' in this part o' the country."

"No," said Wilbur, looking around him, "I guess there isn't."

The road ran along a little gully with a small stream shaded by scrub oak, but arising from this and similar gullies, in great rounded bosses, heaved the barren slopes, the grass already turning yellow and too sparse to cloak the red earth below.

"Yet," said Rifle-Eye, pointing with his finger as he spoke, "there's a desert fox."

Wilbur strained his eyes to see, but the unfamiliar growth of cacti, sage-brush, palo verde, and the dusty-miller plants made quick vision difficult. In a moment, however, he caught sight of the little reddish-gray animal running swiftly and almost indistinguishable from its surroundings.

"But up there?" queried the boy, pointing in front of them. The road wound onward toward the middle Sierras, thickly wooded with oak and digger pine, and, of course, the chapparal, and towering to the clouds rose the mighty serrated peaks of the range, where magnificent forests of pine, fir, and cedar swept upwards to the limits of eternal snow. "Up there the hunting must be wonderful."

"Among the mount'ns!" said the old hunter slowly. "Wa'al, up there, you see, is home."

"You certainly can't complain about the looks of your home, then," said the boy, "for that's just about the finest I've ever seen."

"'There's no place like home,'" quoted Rifle-Eye quietly, "but I ain't ever feelin' that my home's so humble. It ain't a question of its bein' good enough fer me, it's a question o' whether I'm good enough fer it."

"It makes quite a house," said Wilbur, following the old mountaineer's line of thought.

"I've never lived in any smaller house than that," responded Rifle-Eye, "an' I reckon now I never will. There's some I know that boasts of ownin' a few feet o' space shut in by a brick wall. Not for me. My house is as far as my eyes c'n see, an' from the ground to the sky."

Wilbur was silent for a moment, feeling the thrill of Nature in the old man's speech.

"It's to be my home, too," he said gently.

Rifle-Eye smiled at the lad.

"I don't know that I'm quite the oldest inhabitant," he said, "but I sure am the oldest Ranger in the Service, an' all I c'n say is, 'Make yerself to home.'"

"All right," said Wilbur promptly, "I'll take that as an official welcome from the Sierras, and I will. But," he added, "you were going to tell me about your hunting. I should think it would be great sport."

"Son," said Rifle-Eye somewhat sharply, "I never killed a harmless critter 'for sport,' as you call it, in my life."

"But I thought," gasped Wilbur in astonishment, "that you were hunting nearly all the time, before you started in as Ranger."

"So I was," was the quiet reply.

"But—but I don't quite see—" Wilbur stopped lamely.

"I said before," resumed the old hunter, "that I never killed a harmless critter onless I had to. Neither have I. Varmints, o' course, is a different matter. I've shot plenty o' them, an' once in a while I've had ter kill fer food. But just shootin' for the sake o' shootin' is the trick of a coward or a fool or a tenderfoot or a mixture of all three. It's plumb unnecessary, an' it's dead wrong."

"You mean shooting deer and so forth?"

"I mean just that, son, if the shootin's only fer antlers an' what these here greenhorns calls 'trophies.' If venison is needed, why, I ain't got nothin' to say. A man's life is worth more than a deer's when he needs food, but a man's conceit ain't worth more than a deer's life."

"How about bear, then, and trapping for skins?" asked the boy.

"I said 'harmless critters.' Now, a bear ain't harmless, leastways, not as you'd notice it. Bear will take young stock, an' they're particularly partial to young pig, an' down among these here foothills we've been passin' through there's a lot o' shiftless hog-rustlers as depends on pork fer a livin'. As for bearskins, why, o' course you use the pelts. What's the idee o' leavin' them around? It ain't any kind o' good tryin' to spare an animal's feelin's when he's plenty good an' dead. But I've made this here section of the Sierras pretty hot for wolves."

"I heard down at the ranch," the boy remarked, "that you had bagged forty-seven wolves last season."

"I did have a good year," assented the Ranger, "an', of course, I can't give much time to it. But I reckon I've disposed of more'n a thousand wolves in my day, one way and another. An' as I look at it, that's makin' pretty good use of time."

"Are wolves worse than bear?" queried Wilbur surprisedly.

"They do a lot more harm in the long run. Cattlemen reckon that a wolf will get away with about four head a year. Myself, I think that's pressin' the average some; I'd put it at somewhere between two an' three. But it's generally figured at four."

"I didn't know that wolves, lone wolves, would attack cattle."

"It's calves an' yearlin's mostly that they go for. It ain't often that you see a wolf tacklin' anythin' bigger'n a two-year-old. But if you figure that a wolf gets rid o' four head a year, an' inflicts himself on a sufferin' community for a space of about ten years, that's somewhere in the neighborhood o' forty head. A thousand wolves means about forty thousand head of cattle, or pretty nigh a million dollars' worth of stock."

"The beef you've saved by killing wolves," commented Wilbur, "would feed quite a town."

"Forty thousand is a tolerable sized bunch. An' that's without figurin' on the wolf cubs there would have been durin' all those years from the older ones whose matrimonial expectations I disappointed plenty abrupt. An' it makes a pile o' difference to cattlemen to know they c'n send a herd grazin' on the national forest, an' be fairly sure they won't lose much by varmints."

"It surely must," said the boy. "But I hadn't realized that wolves were such a danger."

"I wouldn't go to say that they was dangerous. An old gray wolf, if you corner him, is surly an' savage, an' will fight anythin' at any odds. Out on the Barren Grounds they're bad, but around the Sierras I ain't heard o' them attackin' humans but twice, an' they was children, lost in the woods. I figure the kids had wandered around till they petered out, an' then, when they were exhausted, the wolves got 'em. But I've never heard of a wolf attackin' a man anywhere in the Rockies."

"But I thought wolves ran in packs often."

"Not in the United States, son, so far as I've heard of. I knew a Russian trapper, though, who meandered down this way from Alaska in the early days. He used to spin a lot o' yarns about the Siberian wolves runnin' in packs an' breakfastin' freely off travelers. But he seemed to think that it was the horses the wolves were after chiefly, although they weren't passin' up any toothsome peasant that happened along."

"And do wolves attack horses here, too?"

"Not on the trail, that fashion. But they're some partial to colts."

"How about coyotes?"

"They're mean critters an' they give a pesky lot o' trouble, although they bother sheep more'n cattle. But a few husky dogs will keep coyotes at a distance, though they'll watch a chance an' sneak off with a young lamb or any sheep what is hurt an' has fallen behind the herd. But they don't worry us here such a great deal, they keep mostly to the plains an' the prairie country."

Saying this, the Ranger pulled up at the door of a shack lying a short distance from the road and gave a hail. Immediately there stepped from the door one of the largest women Wilbur had ever seen. Though her hair was gray, and she was angular and harsh of feature, yet, standing well over six feet and quite erect, she seemed to fit in well under the shadow of the Sierras.

"I reckon you've some bacon, Susan?" was the Ranger's greeting as he swung himself off his horse. Wilbur followed suit.

"There's somethin' awful would have to happen to a pile o' hogs," was the reply, "when you came by here an' couldn't get a bite."

By this time a swarm of children had come out, and Wilbur, seeing that the Ranger had simply resigned his horse into the hands of one of the larger boys, did likewise and followed his guide into the house.

"I wasn't sure if I'd find you here, Susan," said the old scout when they were seated at a simple meal. "I thought you were goin' to move into town."

"I did," she replied. "I stayed thar jest two weeks. An' they was two weeks o' misery. These yar towns is too crowded for me. Now, hogs, I've been used to 'em all my life, an' I don't mind how many's around. But it only takes a few folks to make me feel as if I was real crowded."

"Do you prefer hogs to people?" questioned Wilbur, smiling.

"Not one by one, bub, o' course," came the slow reply, "but when it comes to a crowd o' both, I'm kind o' lost with folks. Everybody's busy an' they don't care nothin' about you, an' it makes you-all feel no 'count. An' the noise is bewilderin'. Have you ever been in a city?"

Wilbur admitted that he had.

"Well, then," she said, "ye'll know what I mean. But out here, there's more room, like, an' I know I'm bigger'n my hogs." Following which, Susan launched into a long description of her favorite porkers, which continued almost without cessation until it was time for the two to be on the trail again.

"That's a queer woman," said Wilbur when they were in the saddle again and out of hearing of the shack.

"She's a good one," answered the Ranger. "Her son, by the way, is a member o' the legislature, an' a good lawyer, an' she's made him what he is. But she ain't the city kind."

"Not with all those children," said Wilbur. "She'd have to hire a block to keep them all."

"Those ain't her own children," replied the Ranger, "not a bit of it. If a youngster gits orphaned or laid up she just says 'Pork's plenty, send 'em to me.' An' I generally do. Other folks do, too, an' quite a few o' them hev been brought her by the 'little white lady' you've been hearing about. She's fonder o' children than any woman I ever saw, is Susan. But she won't talk kids, she'll only talk hogs."

"That's pretty fine work, I think," said the boy. "But I should imagine the youngsters wouldn't have much of a chance. It isn't any better than a backwoods life, away out there."

The old Ranger, usually so slow and deliberate in his movements, turned on him like a flash.

"The meanest thing in this world," he said, "is not bein' able to see or willin' to see what some one else has done for you. There ain't a home in all these here United States that don't owe its happiness to the backwoodsman. You can't make a country civilized by sittin' in an office an' writin' the word 'civilized' on the map. Some one has got to get out an' do it, an' keep on doin' it till it's done. It was the man who had nothin' in the world but a wife, a rifle, an' an ax who made America."

"I had forgotten for the moment," said the boy, a little taken off his feet by the sudden energy and the flashing speech of the usually impassive mountaineer.

"So does mighty near every one else 'forget for the moment.' But if the backwoodsman forgot for the moment he was likely to be missin' his scalp-lock, or if he tried to take a holiday it meant his family would go hungry. He never forgot his children or his children's children, but they're none too fond o' rememberin' him.

"Everythin' you have now, he first showed you how. If he wanted a house, he had to build it; if he wanted bread, he had to raise the grain, grind, an' bake it; if he wanted clothin', he had to get skins, cure, an' sew 'em. But he never had to hunt for honor an' for courage; he brought those with him; an' he didn't have to get any book-larnin' to teach him how to make his cabin a home, an' his wife an' his children were allers joys to him, not cares. They were men! An' what do you reckon made 'em men?"

"The hardships of the life, I suppose," hazarded Wilbur.

"Not a bit of it; it was the forest. The forest was their nurse in infancy, their playmate when they were barefooted kids runnin' around under the trees, their work by day, an' their home when it was dark. They lived right down with Nature, an' they larned that if she was rugged, she was kind. They became rugged an' kind, too. An' that's what the right sort of American is to this day."

"A lot of our best statesmen in early days were from the newly cleared settlements; that's a fact," said Wilbur thoughtfully, "right up to the Civil War."

"An' through it!" added the Ranger. "How about Abe Lincoln?"

Wilbur thought to himself that perhaps "backwoodsman" was not quite a fair idea of the great President's Illinois upbringing, but he thought it wiser not to argue the point to no profit.

"But it's all different now," continued Rifle-Eye a trifle sadly, "things have changed an' the city's beginnin' to have a bigger hold than the forest. An' the forest still needs, an' I reckon it allers will need, the old kind o' men. Once we had to fight tooth an' nail agin the forest jest to get enough land to live on, an' now we've got to fight jest as hard for the forest so as there'll be enough of it for what we need. In this here country you can't ever get away from the woods-dweller, whether he's backwoodsman or Forester, or whatever you call him — the man who can depend on himself an' live his life wherever there's sky overhead an' ground underfoot an' trees between.

"They're the discoverers of America, too. Oh, yes, they are," he continued, noting Wilbur's look of contradiction. "It wasn't Columbus or Amerigo or any o' the floatin' adventurers who first saw a blue splotch o' land on the horizon that discovered America. It was the men who conquered the forest, who found all, did all, an' became all that the life demanded, that really brought into bein' America an' the Americans."

The Ranger stopped as suddenly as he had begun, and, touching his horse lightly with the spur, went on ahead up the trail. Evidently he was thinking of the old times and the boy had wisdom enough not to disturb him. As the afternoon drew on the foothills were left behind and the open road became more and more enclosed, until at last it was simply a trail through the forest. The shadows were lengthening and it was drawing on toward evening, when the Ranger halted beside a little ravine, densely wooded with yellow pine, incense cedar, and white fir. Wilbur was tired and his horses, fresh to the trail, were showing signs of fatigue, so he was glad to stop.

"I don't know how you feel about it," said the Ranger, "but I reckon I'll camp here. There's a good spring a couple of hundred feet down stream. But you ain't used to this sort o' thing, an' maybe you'd better keep on the trail for another half-mile till you come to a little settlement. Somebody can put you up, I reckon."

"No need to," said the boy, "I'll camp here with you."

"Maybe you ain't used to sleepin' on the ground."

"I guess I can stand it, if you can," replied Wilbur promptly.

"Wa'al, I reckon I can," said the Ranger, "seein' that I always have an' always do."

Wilbur had never camped in the open before without a tent or shelter of some kind, but he would not for the world have had his Ranger think that he was in the least disconcerted. Neither, to do him justice, was he, but rather anticipating the night under the open sky with a good deal of pleasure.

After the horses were unsaddled and hobbled, Rifle-Eye told Wilbur to get the beds ready. The boy, greatly pleased with himself that he knew how to do this without being told, picked up his ax and started for the nearest balsam. But he found himself in somewhat of a difficulty. The white fir grew to a much larger tree than the Balm-of-Gilead he had known in the East, and the lower branches were tough. So he chopped down a young tree near, scarcely more than a sapling.

A moment later he heard the Ranger call to him.

"How many trees of that size do you reckon you'll want?" he asked.

"Oh, they're only just saplings," the boy replied, "five or six ought to do."

"They'll make five or six fine trees some day, won't they?" queried the old woodsman.

"Yes, Rifle-Eye, they will," answered the boy, flushing at his lack of thoughtfulness. "I'd better take only one, and that a little bigger, hadn't I?"

"An' one that's crooked. Always take a tree that isn't goin' to make good timber when you're not cuttin' for timber."

Wilbur accordingly felled a small white fir near by, having had his first practical lesson of forest economy on his own forest, stripped the tree of its fans or flattest branches and laid them on the ground. A thickness of about six inches, he found, was enough to make the beds wonderfully springy and comfortable.

In the meantime he found that Rifle-Eye was getting a fireplace ready, using for the purpose some flat stones which lay conveniently near by. Wilbur, stepping over a tiny rivulet which ran into the creek, noted a couple of stones apparently just suited for the making of a rough fireplace and brought them along. The Ranger looked at them.

"What kind o' stone do you call that?" he asked.

"Granite," said Wilbur immediately.

"An' you took them out o' the water?"

"Yes," answered the boy.

"An' what happens when you build a fire between granite stones?"

"I don't know, Rifle-Eye. What does?"

"They explode sometimes, leastways, when they're wet inside. Don't forget that," he added as he put the stones aside. "Now," he continued, "go down to the spring an' fill this pot with water, an' I'll have a fire goin' an' some grub sizzlin' by the time you get back. The spring is about two hundred feet downstream and about twenty feet above the water. You can't miss it."

Wilbur took the aluminum pot and started for the spring. He had not gone half the distance when he noted a stout crotched stick such as he had been used to getting when he camped out in the middle West for the purpose of hanging the cooking utensils on over the fire. So he picked it up and carried it along with him. Presently the gurgling of water told him that he was nearing the spring, and a moment later he saw the clearing through the trees. But, suddenly, a low snarling met his ears, and he halted dead at the edge of the clearing.

There, before him, on the ground immediately beside the spring, crouched a large wild-cat, the hairy tips of her ears twitching nervously. Under her claws was a rabbit, evidently just caught, into which the wild-cat had just sunk her teeth when the approach of the boy was heard. At first Wilbur could not understand why she had not sprung into the woods with her prey at the first distant twig-snapping which would betoken his approach. But as he looked more closely he saw that this was precisely what the cat had tried to do, but that in the jerk the rabbit had been caught and partly impaled on a tree root that projected above the ground, and for the moment the cat could not budge it.

Wilbur was utterly at a loss to know what to do. He had been told that wild-cats would never attack any one unless they had been provoked to fight, and he found himself very unwilling to provoke this particular specimen. The cat stood still, her eyes narrowed to mere slits, the ears slightly moving, and the tip of the tail flicking from side to side in quick, angry jerks. There was menace in every line of the wild-cat's pose.

The boy had his revolver with him, but while he had occasionally fired a six-shooter, he was by no means a crack shot, and he realized that if he fired at and only wounded the creature he would unquestionably be attacked. And there was a lithe suppleness in the manner that the movement of the muscles rippled over the skin that was alarmingly suggestive of ferocity. Wilbur did not like the looks of it at all. On the other hand, he had not the slightest intention of going back to the camp without water. He had come for water, and he would carry water back, he thought to himself, if a regiment of bob-cats was in the way.

The old fable that a wild beast cannot stand the gaze of the human eye recurred to Wilbur's remembrance, and he stood at the edge of the clearing regarding the cat fixedly. But the snarls only grew the louder. Wilbur was frightened, and he knew it, and what was more, he felt the cat knew it with that intuition the wild animals have for recognizing danger or the absence of danger. She made another effort to drag away the rabbit, but failing in that, with an angry yowl, with quick jerks and rending of her powerful jaws began to try to force the rabbit free from the entangling root, which done, she could carry it into the forest to devour at leisure. The ease with which those claws and teeth rent asunder the yielding flesh was an instructive sight for Wilbur, but the fact that the wild-cat should dare to go on striving to free her prey instead of slinking away in fright made the boy angry. Besides, he had come for that water.

Wilbur decided to advance into the clearing anyway, and then, if the creature did not stir, he would be so near that he couldn't miss her with the revolver. As he grew angrier his fear began to leave him. He took the pot in his left hand, putting the long stick under his arm, and, drawing his six-shooter, advanced on the cat. He came forward slowly, but without hesitation. At his second step forward the wild-cat raised her head, but instead of springing at him, as Wilbur half feared, she retreated into the woods, leaving her prey, snarling as she went. Wilbur went boldly forward to the spring, and, thinking that he would see no more of the cat, put away his revolver.

Having secured the water, and as he turned to go, however, the boy felt a sudden impulse to look up. He had not heard a sound, and yet, on a low branch a few feet above his head, crouched the wild-cat, her eyes glaring yellow in the waning light. Once again he felt the temptation to shoot her, but resisted it, through his fear of only wounding the creature and thus bringing her full fury upon him.

But it occurred to Wilbur that it was not unlikely that he might have to come back to the spring a second time for more water, and he did not wish to risk another encounter. He thought to himself that if he did return and interrupted the wild-cat a second time he would not escape as easily as he had on this occasion, and consequently he tried to devise a means to prevent such meeting. He figured that if he picked up the rabbit and threw it far into the woods the cat would follow and the path to the spring would be open. Forgetting for the moment that he could not expect the angry creature in the tree to divine the honesty of his intentions, he stooped down and grasped the rabbit by the leg to throw it into the forest. As he did so, the wild-cat, thinking herself about to be deprived of her prey, sprang at him.

With one hand holding the pot of water, which, boy-like, he did not want to spill, and the other grasping the rabbit, Wilbur was terribly handicapped. But, by the greatest good fortune, as he stooped, the crotch of the stick that he was carrying caught the wild-cat under the body as she launched herself at him from the tree. The stick was knocked out of the boy's grasp, but it also turned the cat aside, and she half fell, landing on Wilbur's outstretched leg, instead of on his neck, which was the objective point in her spring. As her claws ripped into the soft flesh of his thigh, Wilbur released his hold of the rabbit, drew his revolver, and fired full at the creature hanging on his leg.

Almost instantaneously with the shot, however, one of her foreclaws shot out and caught the back of his right hand, making a long but superficial gash from the wrist to the knuckles. At the same time, too, one of her hind claws struck down, opening the calf of the leg and making the boy sick for a moment. His right hand was bleeding vigorously and paining a good deal, but his finger was still on the trigger and Wilbur fired again. A moment later, the Ranger came running into the clearing. But before he reached the boy's side the cat had fallen limply to the ground. The second shot had gone clear through her skull, and, being fired at point-blank distance, had almost blown her head off.

The old Ranger, without wasting time in words, quickly examined the boy's injuries and found them slight, although they were bleeding profusely. Wilbur reached out the pot full of water from the spring.

"Here's the water, Rifle-Eye," he said a little quaveringly; "I hardly spilled a drop."

The old woodsman took the vessel without a word. Then he looked down at the cat.

"Just as well for you," he said, "that it wasn't a true lynx. But how did she get at your leg? Did you walk on her, or kick her, just for fun?"

Wilbur, laughing a little nervously from the reaction of the excitement, described how it was that the wild-cat had landed on his leg instead of on his neck, and the old hunter nodded.

"It's a mighty lucky thing for you," he said, "that stick was there, because there's a heap o' places around the neck where a clawin' ain't healthy. But these scratches of yours won't take long to heal. Where you were a fool," he continued, "was in touchin' the rabbit at all. It's just as I told you. When you went quietly forward, you say, the bob-cat got out of your road all right. Of course, that's what she ought to do. And if you had filled the pot with water an' come away that's all there'd have been to it. But jest as soon as you begin ter get mixed up in the prey any varmint's killed, you've got ter begin considerin' the chances o' joinin' the select company o' victims."

"But I wanted her out of the way for next time," said Wilbur.

"She'd have got out of your way so quick you couldn't see her go," said the hunter, "if you'd given her a chance. Next time, leave a varmint's dinner alone."

"Next time, I will," the boy declared.

"I guess now," continued the old hunter, "you'd better come back to camp an' we'll see what we c'n do to improve them delicate attentions you've received. An' don't be quite the same kind of an idiot again."

"Well," said Wilbur, "I got the water from the spring, anyhow."

CHAPTER VI
IN THE HEART OF THE FOREST

Towards noon the next day, Wilbur and the Ranger rode up to the shack in the woods which Rifle-Eye considered as one of his headquarters. As soon as they reached the clearing they were met by a big, shambling youth, whose general appearance and hesitating air proclaimed him to be the half-witted lad of whom Wilbur had heard. He came forward and took the horses.

"You've heard about Ben?" queried the hunter as the horses were being led away.

"Yes," answered Wilbur, "Bob-Cat Bob told me all about the death of his father during the sheep and cattle war. He told me when we were riding up to the ranch, from the station at Sumber."

"I have thought," said Rifle-Eye, "that perhaps it ain't quite the right thing to keep Ben here, up in the woods. But I tried sendin' him to school. It wasn't no manner of use. It only troubled the teacher an' bothered him, an' I reckon his life will stack up at the end jest as well, even if he can't read."

"What does he do while you are away?" asked Wilbur.

"Oh, a lot of things. He ain't idle a minute, really, an' there's times that he's as good as them that thinks themselves so wise."

"What sort of things?"

"Well, he's done a lot o' work stampin' out the prairie dogs. Of course, there's very few o' them in these parts, so few that the government has made no appropriation for this forest. It's in Eastern Montana an' the Dakotas that you get them, an' there's been a lot o' trouble in the Custer an' Sioux forests. He's gone there several times, an' there's been villages o' them here among the foothills that Ben's cleared up entirely."

"They poison the prairie dogs, don't they?"

"Yes, with strychnine, mainly. Grain is soaked in the poison an' a few grains put outside each hole in a dog town. If this is done early in the year, before the green grass is up for food, it will pretty nearly clean up the town."

"It seems rather a shame," said Wilbur, "they are such fat, jolly little fellows, and the way they sit up on their hind legs and look at you is a wonder."

"It's all right for them to look 'fat and jolly,'" replied Rifle-Eye, "but when the stock raiser finds hundreds of acres of grass nibbled down to the roots, an' when the farmer's young wheat is ruined, they don't see so much jollity in it."

"But I didn't know that the Forest Service took a hand in that sort of thing."

"Only indirectly. But they provide the poison an' the settlers usually git some one to put it round. As I say, Ben's been doin' a lot of it this spring."

"But that sort of work doesn't last long."

"No, only in the spring. But Ben's busy other ways. Sometimes he goes down to the valleys an' helps the ranchers with their hayin'. He don't know anythin' about money, though, an' so they never pay him cash."

"That's tough on Ben, then," remarked Wilbur. "Does he work all the time for nothing?"

"Not at all. They always see that he gits a fair return. Every once in a while the man he's workin' for will drive up to the shack with some bacon an' a barrel o' flour an' trimmin's. Often as not, he'll bring the wife along, an' she'll go over the lad's things to find what he needs."

"That's mighty nice," commented Wilbur.

"Some of 'em are as good to Ben as if he was their own," said the Ranger. "They'll go over everything he's got, fix up whatever needs mendin', an' make a list o' things to be bought next time any one goes into town. You see, he gits his wages that way. He works well, an' so it ain't like charity, an' at the same time it gives the man he works for a chance to do the right thing."

"I suppose if he didn't, you'd get after him," suggested the boy.

"Never had to yet, an' never expect to," was the prompt reply. "Mostly folks is all right, an' a lot o' the supposed selfishness is jest because they ain't been reminded. And then Ben never makes trouble."

"He seems quiet enough," said Wilbur, with a gesture towards the doorway where the lad was approaching. He came in and stood looking vacantly at the two sitting together.

"What were you doin' yesterday, Ben?" asked the Ranger sharply to rouse him.

The lad flung out both arms with a wild gesture.

"I was away, away, far away," he answered; "away, away over the hills."

"Where?"

The half-witted lad passed his hand across his eyes.

"With Mickey," he said.

"An' what were you an' Mickey doin'?"

"Lots of things, lots, lots, lots. Little fires creep, creep, creepin' on the ground," he moved his hands waveringly backward and forward as though to show the progress of the flames, "then put them out quick, so!" he stamped his foot on the ground.

"Does he mean a forest fire, Rifle-Eye?" queried Wilbur, alert at the very mention of fire.

"No, no, no," interrupted Ben; "little bit fires. Pile burn, burn hot, grass catch fire, put out grass."

"You mean," said the mountaineer, "that you an' Mickey were burnin' up brush?"

"Yes, brush all in piles, burn."

"It's a pretty risky business," said Rifle-Eye, "this burnin' brush in the late spring, but Mickey's right enough to have had Ben along. He's one o' the best fire-fighters that ever happened. He never knows enough to quit."

"Did you have any trouble, Ben?" asked Wilbur.

"One little fire, walk, walk, walk away into the woods. But I stopped him."

"Alone?"

The half-witted lad nodded. Then, coming over to Wilbur, he pointed to the rude bandages and said questioningly:

"Tumble?"

"No, Ben," replied the other boy, "I got into a mix-up with a bob-cat."

"I fight, too. Wait, I show you something."

He disappeared for a moment and then came back with two wolf pups, carrying one in each hand as he might a kitten.

"I got five more," he said.

"Where did you get 'em, Ben?" asked the Ranger.

"Way, way over. Deadman Canyon."

"Get the old wolf?"

The half-witted lad nodded his head vigorously several times.

"Yes," he said, "dead, dead, dead."

"Was the den just by the Sentinel Pine?"

"Yes."

"I reckon that's the wolf that's been givin' such a lot of trouble on the Arroyo," commented Rifle-Eye. "I went out after that wolf one day this spring, Ben, but I didn't get her. I waited at the den a long time, too."

"Two holes out of den, two. I wait, too. Long, long time. No come out. Plug up one hole. Long more time waited. Then wolf go in. I go in, too."

"You went into the wolf's den?" queried Wilbur in amazement.

"Yes, in. Far, far in."

"How far?"

"Don't know. Far."

"Well, I went in about forty feet myself," said the old hunter, "an' I didn't see any sign o' the pups, so I backed out again. If you went all the way in, Ben, I reckon it was a pretty long crawl."

"But why did you go in the den when the mother wolf was there?" asked Wilbur.

"Boy fool," said the half-witted lad, pointing at him. "Why go in if wolf not there?"

"Well," said Wilbur, on the defensive, "I should think it a whole lot safer to go in — that is, if I was going in at all — sometime when I'd be sure the mother wolf wouldn't be there."

But the other, still holding the cubs in his hands, negatived this reasoning with a vigorous shake of the head.

"Safer, wolf in," he said.

"I don't see that at all," objected Wilbur. "It can't be safer."

"You go in, in far, when wolf out. By and by wolf come, eat up legs, no can turn round for shoot."

"I hadn't thought of that," the boy said, a little humbled.

"Ben's nearly right," said the Ranger, "an' it ain't really as dangerous as it sounds. There ain't room in the passage for the wolf to spring, an' if you shoot you're bound to hit her somewhere, no matter how you aim. O' course, a wolf ain't goin' to come along an' 'eat up your legs' the way he puts it, but you might get a nasty bite or two. It's a lot better to go after a wolf than have the wolf come after you. It takes more nerve, but it ain't so hard at that."

"But how did you kill the old wolf, Ben?" asked Wilbur.

"I go in, far in. See eyes glitter. Shoot once. Shoot twice. Old wolf dead. Take out pups, easy. Skin wolf."

"Where's the skin?"

"Dryin'."

But Wilbur was by no means satisfied and he plied the half-witted lad with questions until he had secured all the details of the story. In the meantime the Ranger had been getting dinner, and as soon as it was over Wilbur was glad to lie down on Ben's bed, for he had lost not a little blood in his tussle with the wild-cat the night before, and riding all morning with those deep scratches only rudely bandaged had been rather a strain. By the time that Rifle-Eye was ready to start again Wilbur was fairly stiffened up, and at the Ranger's suggestion he agreed to stay on a couple of days in the shack, having Ben cook for him and look after him, as the Ranger felt that he himself ought to get back to headquarters.

It was not until the third day that Wilbur once more got into the saddle and with Ben to guide him through the forest, started for the Supervisor's headquarters, or rather the Ranger's cabin where the Supervisor was staying. The two boys rode on and up, leaving behind the scrub oak, chapparal, and manzanita, and into the great yellow pine and sugar pine forests. Shortly before noontime they heard voices in the woods, and Ben, after listening a moment, turned from the trail. In a few minutes he reined up beside a tall, sunburned man, walking through the woods pencil and notebook in hand. At the same time the Ranger, who was working with him, stepped up.

"Thanks, Ben," he said. Then, turning to the Supervisor, he said: "Merritt, here's the boy!"

Wilbur's new chief stepped forward quickly and held out his hand with a word of greeting. Wilbur shook it heartily and decided on the spot that he was going to like him. Wearing khaki with the Forest Service bronze badge, a Stetson army hat, and the high lace boots customarily seen, he looked thoroughly equipped for business.

"You're Wilbur Loyle," he said, "of course. I heard you were coming. Have you had any experience?"

"Just the Colorado Ranger School, sir," said the boy.

"You were to be here three days ago."

"Yes, Mr. Merritt, but I was delayed, and I put up a couple of days with Ben, here."

"He reckoned he had more right to a rabbit what a bob-cat was feastin' on than the cat had," volunteered Rifle-Eye in explanation. "In the ensooin' disagreement he got a bit scratched, an' so I looked after him. I told him to stay at Ben's, an' I guess he's all right now."

"Being three days late isn't the best start in the world," said the Supervisor sharply, "but if Rifle-Eye knows all about it and is willing to stand for it, I won't say any more. Can you cruise?"

"I've learned, sir, but I haven't done much of it. I think, though, I can do it, all right."

"Very well. We'll break off for dinner now, and you can try this afternoon. Or do you still feel tired, and would you rather wait until to-morrow?"

"Thanks, Mr. Merritt," answered Wilbur, "but I want to start right now."

"Very well," said the Supervisor laconically. Then, turning to the Ranger, he commenced talking with him about the work in hand, and for the moment Wilbur was left aside. The lumberman who had been working on the other side of the Supervisor, however, sauntered up and introduced himself as "McGinnis, me boy, Red McGinnis, they call me, because of the natural beauty of me hair."

"I'm very glad, Mr. McGinnis—" began the boy when the lumberman interrupted him.

"'Tis very sorry ye'll be if ye call me out of me right name. Sure I said McGinnis, jest plain McGinnis, not Misther McGinnis. Ye can call me 'Judge,' or 'Doctor,' or 'Colonel,' or annything else, but I won't be called Misther by annyone."

"Very well, McGinnis," said the boy, looking at his height and broad shoulders, "I guess there's no one that will make you."

"There is not!" the big lumberman replied. "And are ye goin' to join us in a little promenade through the timber?"

"So Mr. Merritt said."

71

"I don't see what for," the Irishman replied. "Sure, there's the three of us now."

"Is there much of it to do?"

"There is that. There's three million feet wanted, half sugar pine and half yellow pine, in this sale alone. An' there's another sale waiting, so I hear, as soon as this one's through."

"Maybe it's just to find out whether I can do it?" suggested Wilbur.

The lumberman nodded affirmatively.

"That's just about it," he said. "Because ye'll have a big stretch to cover as Guard, an' there'll be no time for ye cruisin'. You keep the trees from burnin' up so as we can mark them for cuttin' down."

"It always seems a shame," said Wilbur, "to have to cut down these trees. Of course, I know it's done so as to help the forest, not to hurt it, and that if the big trees weren't cut down the young ones couldn't get sunlight and wouldn't have a chance to grow. But still one hates to see a big tree go."

"It isn't that way at all, at all," said the lumberman. "There's some that does their best work livin', and there's some that does it dead. A man does it livin' and a tree does it dead. But what a tree does after it's dead depends on what kind of a chance it's had when it's been livin'. Sure ye've been to the schools when all the girls and some of the boys gets into white dresses, the girls I mean, and sings songs, and gives speeches and class poems and other contraptions, and graduates."

"I have," said Wilbur, "and not so long ago at that."

"And so have I," answered the lumberman. "Sure, me own little Kathleen was graduated just a month ago from high school. Well, cuttin' down a tree is like its graduation. It's been livin' and growin' and gettin' big and strong and makin' up into good timber. Now its schoolin' in the forest is over, it's goin' out into the world, to be made useful in some kind of way, and in goin' it makes room for more."

"You don't take kindly to the 'Oh, Woodman, spare that tree' ideal?" smiled Wilbur.

"I do not. But I'd spare it, all right, until there were other young trees growin' near it to take its place in time. 'Tis the biggest part of the work is cuttin' down the trees that make the best timber."

When they were settled drinking hot tea and eating some trout that the party had with them, the Supervisor turned to Wilbur.

"McGinnis is a good man," he began, smiling as the Irishman with pantomime returned the compliment by drinking his health in a pannikin of tea, "but he's so built that he can't see straight. If you introduce McGinnis to a girl he'll want to estimate how many feet she'd make board measure."

He dodged a pine cone which the Irishman threw at him.

"How about Aileen?" he said.

"I'll take that back," said Merritt; "Mrs. McGinnis hasn't gone to diameter growth. But," he continued, "she's good on clear length and has a fine crown."

By which Wilbur readily understood that the lumberman's wife was slight, well-built, and neat, and with heavy hair. The lumberman, mollified by the tribute, returned to his dinner, and the Supervisor continued:

"McGinnis told you that cutting down the best trees available for timber is the most important part of forest work. It's not. The most important thing is keeping the forest at its best. Cutting trees when they have reached their maximum is a most necessary part, and it's a policy that helps to make the forest pay for itself. But the value to the forest lies in its conservation. You know about that?"

"Yes, sir," said the boy; "it's keeping the watersheds from becoming deforested, either by cutting or by fire, and so preventing erosion from taking place."

"I reckon," put in the old Ranger, "thar's another that pleases me still better than either of those."

"And what's that, Rifle-Eye?" asked Merritt.

"It's the plantin'. When I walk along some of the forest nurseries, an' see hundreds and hundreds of little seedlin's all growin' protected like, and bein' cared for just the same as if they was little children, an' when I know that in fifty years time they'll be big fine trees like the one we're sittin' under, I tell you it looks pretty good to me. They're such helpless little things, seedlin's, and they do have such a time to get a start. Nursery's a good name all right. I've been along some of 'em at night, when the moonlight was a shinin' down on them, and they wasn't really no different from children in their little beds."

"I should think," said Wilbur, "that the changing of a forest from one kind of tree to another would be the most interesting. I mean getting rid of the worthless trees and giving the advantage to those that are finer."

"And a few sections west," commented the Supervisor, "you would find that Bellwall, who's the Ranger there, thinks that the most interesting thing in the whole of the forest work is putting an end to the diseases of trees and to the insects that are a danger to them. Another Ranger may be a tree surgeon."

"A tree surgeon doesn't help so much," put in McGinnis, "the timber is niver worth a whoop!"

"There you go again," said the head of the forest, "there's other things to be thought of besides timber." He turned to the boy. "You don't know the trees of the Sierras, I suppose?"

"I think I know them pretty well now," answered Wilbur. "I had to learn a lot about them at school, and then Rifle-Eye has been giving me pointers the last few days."

"What's the difference between a yellow pine and a sugar pine?" queried the Supervisor.

"Sugar pine wood is white and soft," said the boy, "yellow pine is hard, harder than any other pine except the long-leaf variety."

"That's right enough. But how are you going to tell them when standing?"

Wilbur thought for a moment.

"I should think," he said, "that the yellow pine is a so much bigger tree as a rule that you could tell it by that alone. But I suppose a younger yellow pine might look like a sugar. The leaves would help, though, because I should think the sugar, like most of the soft pines, has its leaves in clusters of five in a sheath, and the yellow being a hard pine, has them in bundles of three."

"How about the bark?"

"Sugar pine bark is smoother," said the boy.

The Supervisor nodded.

"All right," he said, "we'll try you at it. You go along with McGinnis for an hour or so, to see just how he does it, and then you can take one side, and he the other. Just for a day or two, while Rifle-Eye looks after some other matters."

Wilbur accordingly took a pair of calipers and walked with McGinnis back to where he had originally met the party. Resuming work the lumberman started through the forest, calling as he went the kind of trees and their approximate size. As, however, this particular portion of the forest had never been "cruised," McGinnis not only called and marked the trees which were to be cut in the sale, but also the other timber.

Thus he would call, as he reached a tree, "Sugar, thirty-four, six," by which Wilbur understood him to mean that the tree was a sugar pine, that it was thirty-four inches in diameter breast high, and that it would cut into six logs of the regular sixteen-foot length. It probably would be thirty or fifty feet higher, but the top could only be used for posts, cordwood, and similar uses. Such a tree, having been estimated and adjudged fit for sale, the lumberman would make a blaze with a small ax, by slicing off a portion of bark about eight inches long, then turning the head of the ax, whereon was "U. S." in raised letters, he would whack the blaze, making a mark which was unchangeable. No other trees than those so marked might be cut.

But as other trees were passed which were not good enough for merchantable timber, he would call these rapidly, "Cedar, small," "Engelmann (spruce), eighteen," "Douglas (spruce), fourteen," all of which were entered by the Supervisor, walking behind, in his cruising book. At the same time he made full notes as to the condition of the young forest, the presence of parasitic plants such as mistletoe, of diseased trees, if any were found, of the nature of the soil, of the drainage of the forest, and of the best way in which the timber sale was to be logged in order to do the least possible damage to the forest.

In a half an hour or so Wilbur dropped back to the Supervisor.

"I think, sir," he said, "that I can do that without any trouble. But I can't do it as fast as McGinnis, sir, for he can tell the size of a tree just by looking at it. I shall have to use the calipers for a day or two."

Merritt looked at him.

"For a day or two?" he said. "McGinnis has been doing it for thirty years. In these Western forests, too. You take him to an Eastern forest and even now he wouldn't be sure of estimating correctly. You use the calipers for a year or two!"

Wilbur, accordingly, quickened his pace, and, going along a little to the left and in advance of the Supervisor, took up his share of the work. He found that he had to depend entirely upon McGinnis for his compass direction, and that he was only doing about one tree to McGinnis' six, but still every hour that passed by gave him greater confidence. The afternoon was wearing away when suddenly they came to a part of the forest in which some timber seemed to have been cut during the winter preceding. McGinnis dropped back.

"Sure, ye didn't tell me that any of this had been cut over," he said aggrievedly.

"It hasn't, so far as I know," said Merritt. He put his book in his pocket and walked on briskly for a few hundred yards. Although the logging had been done the preceding winter the signs were clear for those who could read them determining the direction in which the logs had been taken.

"That's Peavey Jo's work," said the Supervisor at last. "I reckon this is where he begins to find trouble on his hands. We'll find out, McGinnis, how much of this timber he has stolen, measure up the stumps and make him pay for every stick he's taken."

"Ye'd better leave Peavey Jo alone. They used to call him 'The Canuck Brute,'" remarked McGinnis.

"He will pay," repeated Merritt quietly, "for every foot that he's got. And I'll see that he does."

"You'll have the fight of your life."

"What of it! You don't want to back out?"

"Back out? Me? I will not! But it'll be a jim-dandy of a scrap."

The Supervisor turned to Wilbur.

"Measure," he said, "the diameter of all those stumps and mark with a bit of chalk those you have measured. We'll talk to Peavey Jo in a day or two."

CHAPTER VII
WILBUR IN HIS OWN CAMP

"I should think," said Wilbur at headquarters that night, when the timber theft of Peavey Jo was being discussed, "that it would be mighty hard to prove that the timber had been taken."

"Why?" asked the Supervisor.

"Well, we can see how the logs were drawn, and so forth, but you can't bring those driveways into court very well, and put them before the judge as Exhibit A, or anything?"

"You could bring affidavits, couldn't you? But there are few who want to go to law about it. A man knows he can't buck the government on a fake case. We have very little trouble now, but there used to be a lot of it."

"Did you ever have to use weapons, Mr. Merritt?" asked the boy, remembering the story he had heard in Washington about the tie-cutters.

"No," was the instant reply. "You don't handle people with a gun any more in California than you do in New York. These aren't the days of Forty-nine."

"But I thought the 'old-timers' still carried guns," persisted the boy.

"Very few do now. But I got into trouble once, or thought I was going to, when I was a Ranger in the Gunnison Forest. It involved some Douglas fir telephone poles. This trespass was done while I was in town for a while in the Supervisor's office. When I came back I happened to pass by this man's camp, and seeing a lot of telephone poles, I asked if they had been cut in the forest. The man was a good deal of a bully, and he ordered me off the place. He said he didn't have to answer any questions, and wasn't going to."

"Did you go?" asked Wilbur.

"Certainly I went. What would be the use of staying around there? But before I left I got a kind of an answer. He said he had shipped in these telephone poles from another part of the State."

"Sure, that was a fairy tale," said McGinnis.

"Of course it was. I went into the forest and searched around, although there had been a recent fall of snow, until I found the place where most of the poles had been cut. Then I went back to the trespasser and told him, saying I would prove to him that it was on government ground.

"He agreed, and we rode to the place. He took his Winchester along and carried it over his shoulder. He wasn't carrying it in the usual way, but had his hand almost level with his shoulder so that the barrel pointed in my direction. I noticed, too, that he was playing with the trigger. It seemed likely that it might suit his purposes rather well if I was accidentally killed. But each time I cantered up close to him, the barrel returned to its natural position.

"Presently, as we rode along, we came to a waterfall, not a big one, but falling with quite a splashing, and under the cover of the noise I suddenly came to a quick gallop, overtook the trespasser, and, grasping his Winchester firmly with both hands, jerked it out of his grasp."

"Sure, he must have been the maddest thing that iver happened!" said McGinnis.

"He was sore, all right. But what could he do? I had the rifle, and we neither of us had any six-shooters. I showed him that there was no object in my shooting him, while he would gain by shooting me, so I proposed to hold the gun. And hold it I did. On my return I put a notice of seizure on the poles.

"The report went through the usual way to the Commissioner of the General Land Office. He wrote me a letter direct about the case and put it up to me to ask the trespasser what proposition of settlement he intended to make. I thought the town was the best place for this and waited at the post-office for a day or two until he came in. There I tackled him, and told him he would have to notify the Department immediately. At this, he and his son invited me outside to fight it out. I told them I did not intend to fight, but that if within thirty minutes they did not make a proposition of settlement I would telegraph to the Department and his case would become one for harsher measures.

"The postmaster set out to convince him that Uncle Sam was too big a job for him to handle, and in twenty minutes or so back he came with an offer which was forwarded to the Department. A year or so later the case was settled by a Special Agent."

McGinnis added several similar stories of timber difficulties, and, supper being over, they got ready to turn in. The headquarters was a most comfortable house, fairly large, having been built by the previous Ranger, who was married. It was now used by another Ranger, as well as Rifle-Eye, being near the borders of their two districts, and having plenty of good water and good feed near. But although it was barely dark, Wilbur was tired enough to be glad to stretch himself on the cot in the little room and sink to sleep amid the soughing of the wind through the pine needles of neighboring forest giants one and two hundred feet high.

Early the next morning, Wilbur tumbled up, went out and looked after his horses, and came in hungry to breakfast.

"I had intended," said the Supervisor, "to go with you this morning and show you the part of the range you are to look after. But I want to get at Peavey Jo, lest he should decide to leave suddenly, and Rifle-Eye will show you the way instead. I had the tent pitched three or four days ago, when you ought to have been here. You'll find that to cover your range takes about six hours' good riding a day. Use a different horse, of course, each day, and remember that your horse in some ways is fully as important as you are. You can stand a heap of things that he can't. A man will tire out any animal that breathes."

"And what have I to do?"

"You have three trails to ride, on three successive days, so that you will have a chance of seeing all your range, or points that will command all your range at least twice a week. And, of course, quite a good deal of it you will cover daily. You are to watch out for fires, and if you see one, put it out. If you can't put it out alone, ride back to your camp and telephone here, as soon as it is evening. Sometimes it is better to keep working alone until you know there's some one to answer the 'phone, sometimes it's better to get help right away. You can tell about that when you have got to the fire and have seen what it is."

Wilbur nodded.

"That's easy enough to follow," he said.

"If a heavy rain comes, you had better ride back here, because for a few days after a big rain a fire isn't likely to start, and there's always lots of other stuff to be done in the forest, trail-building, and things of that sort."

"Very well, Mr. Merritt," answered the boy.

"There are no timber sales going on in that section of the forest, so that if you see any cutting going on, just ride up quietly and get into conversation with the people cutting and casually find out their names. Ask no other questions, but in the evening telephone to me."

"The telephone must be a big convenience. But," added Wilbur, "it seems to take away the primitiveness of it, somehow."

"Wilbur," said the Supervisor seriously, "you don't want to run into the mistake of thinking that life on a national forest is principally a picturesque performance. It's a business that the government is running for the benefit of the country at large. Anything that can be done to make it efficient is tremendously important. The telephone already has saved many a fearful night ride through bad places of the forest, has been the means of stopping many a fire, and has saved many a life in consequence. I think that's a little more important than 'primitiveness,' as you call it."

The boy accepted the rebuke silently. Indeed, there was nothing more to say.

"As for grazing, there's not much to be said, except that the sheep limits are pretty well defined. The cattle can wander up the range without doing much harm here, for the young forest is of pretty good growth, but the sheep must stay down where they belong. Rifle-Eye will show you where, and sheep notices have been posted all along the limits. And if there's anything you don't know, ask. And I guess that's about all."

The Supervisor rose to go, but Wilbur stopped him.

"How am I to arrange about supplies?" he said.

"The tent's near a spring," was the brief but all-embracing reply. "There's a lake near by with plenty of trout, there's flour and groceries and canned stuff in a cache, and the Guard that was there last year had some kind of a little garden. You can see what there is, and if you want seeds of any kind, let me know. And there's nothing to prevent you shooting rabbits, though they're not much good this time of year."

"I'll get along all right, Mr. Merritt," said Wilbur confidently.

"I'll ride over on Sunday and see you anyway," added the Supervisor as he strode through the doorway, meeting McGinnis, who was waiting for him outside. Wilbur followed him to the door.

"'Tis all the luck in the world I'm wishin' ye," shouted the big Irishman, "an' while ye're keepin' the fires away we'll be gettin' another nicely started for that old logjammer. Sure, we'll make it hot enough for him."

"Good hunting," responded Wilbur with a laugh, as the two men disappeared under the trees.

Although only a day had passed since Wilbur had met the Supervisor and McGinnis, it seemed to him that several days must have elapsed, so much had happened, and he found it hard to believe, when he found himself in the saddle again beside the old Ranger, that they had started from Ben's shack only the morning before.

"I like Mr. Merritt," he said as soon as they had got started. "I like McGinnis, too."

"I reckon he wasn't over-pleased with your bein' late?" queried Rifle-Eye.

"He wasn't," admitted the boy candidly, "but I don't blame him for that. I liked him just the same. But I don't think it's safe to monkey with him. Now, McGinnis is easygoing and good-natured."

"So is a mountain river runnin' down a smooth bed. The river is just the same old river when rocks get in the road, but it acts a lot different. Now, Merritt, when he's satisfied and when he ain't, don't vary, but I tell you, McGinnis can show white water sometimes."

"I don't think I'm aching to be that rock," said Wilbur with a grin.

"Wa'al," said the Ranger, "I ain't filed no petition for the nomination, not yet."

"But tell me, Rifle-Eye," said the boy, "what is McGinnis? He isn't a Guard, is he? and he doesn't talk like a Ranger from another part of the forest."

"No, he's an expert lumberman," replied the hunter. "He isn't attached to this forest at all. He ain't even under the service of the government all the while. He generally is, because he knows his business an' the Forest Service knows a good man when it sees one. They engage him for a month, or three, or four months, an' he goes wherever there's a timber sale, or a big cut. Often as not, he teaches the Rangers a heap of things they don't know about lumberin', and the Forest Assistants themselves ain't above takin' practical pointers from him."

"But I thought Mr. Merritt said that McGinnis only knew this kind of forest?"

"He said McGinnis wouldn't know anything of an Eastern hardwood forest. That's right. But the government hasn't got any hardwood forests yet, though I guess they soon will in the Appalachians. But you can't lose him in any kind of pine. I've met up with him from Arizona to Alaska."

The old woodsman turned sharply from the trail, apparently into the unbroken forest.

"Do you see the trail?" he asked.

Wilbur looked on the ground to see if he could discern any traces. Not doing so, he looked up at the Ranger, who had half turned in the saddle to watch him. As he shook his head in denial he noticed the old mountaineer looking at him with grieved surprise.

"What do you reckon you were lookin' on the ground for?" he asked.

"For the trail," said Wilbur.

"Did ye think this was a city park?" said Rifle-Eye disgustedly.

"Well, I never saw a trail before that you couldn't see," responded Wilbur defiantly.

The old hunter stopped his horse.

"Turn half round," he said. Wilbur did so. "Now," he continued, "can you see any trail through there?"

The boy looked through the long cool aisles of trees, realizing that he could ride in any direction without being stopped by undergrowth, but he could see nothing that looked like a trail.

"Now turn round and look ahead," said the hunter.

The moment Wilbur turned he became conscious of what the old mountaineer wanted to show him. Not a definite sign could he see, the ground was untrampled, the trees showed no blaze marks, yet somehow there was a consciousness that in a certain direction there was a way.

"Yes," he said vaguely. "I can't see it, but I feel somehow that there's a trail through there." He pointed between two large spruces that stood near.

The hunter slapped his pony on the neck.

"Get up there, Milly," he said, "we'll teach him yet! You see," he continued, "there ain't no manner of use in tryin' to see a trail. If the trail's visible, the worst tenderfoot that ever lived could follow it. It's the trail that you can't see that you've got to learn to follow."

"And how do you do it, Rifle-Eye?" asked the boy.

"Same as you did just now. There's just a mite of difference where folks have ridden, there's perhaps just a few seedlin's been trodden down, an' there's a line between the trees that's just a little straighter than any animal's runway. But it's so faint that the more you think about it, the less sure you are. But, by an' by, you get so that you couldn't help followin' it in any kind of weather." And the old hunter, seeing the need of teaching

Wilbur the intricacies of the pine country forests, gave him hint after hint all the way to his little camp.

When he got there Wilbur gave an exclamation of delight. The camp, as the Supervisor had said, was near a little spring, which indeed bubbled from the hillside not more than ten feet away from the tent, and gleaming on the slope a couple of hundred feet below, he could see the little lake which was "so full of trout" glistening itself like a silver fish in the sunlight. A tall flagstaff, with a cord all reeved for the flag, stood by the tent, and for the realities of life a strong, serviceable telephone was fastened to a tree.

Wilbur turned to the hunter, his eyes shining.

"What a daisy place!" he cried.

The old hunter smiled at his enthusiasm.

"Let's see the tent," he said, and was about to leap from his horse when the hunter called him.

"I reckon, son," he said, "there's somethin' you're forgettin'."

"What's that?" said Wilbur.

"Horses come first," said Rifle-Eye. "It's nigh dinner-time now. Where's the corral?"

But Wilbur's spirits were not to be dampened by any check.

"Is there a corral?" he said. "How bully! Oh, yes, I remember now Mr. Merritt said there was. Where is it, Rifle-Eye? Say, this is a jim-dandy of a camp!"

A few steps further they came to the corral, a pretty little meadow in a clearing, and in the far corner of it the stream which trickled from the spring near the house. Wilbur unsaddled with a whoop and turned the horses in the corral, then hurried back to the camp. The old hunter, thinking perhaps that the boy would rather have the feeling of doing it all himself for the first time, had not gone near the tent. There was a small outer tent, which was little more than a strip of canvas thrown over a horizontal pole and shielding a rough fireplace for rainy weather, and within was the little dwelling-tent, with a cot, and even a tiny table. On the ground was Wilbur's pack, containing all the things he had sent up when he had broken his journey to go to the Double Bar J ranch, and there, upon the bed, all spread out in the fullness of its glory, was a brand-new Stars and Stripes. For a moment the boy's breath was taken away, then, with a dash, he rushed for it, and fairly danced out to the flagpole, where he fastened it and ran it to the truck, shouting as he did so. His friend, entering into the boy's feelings, solemnly raised his hat, as the flag settled at the peak and waved in the wind. Wilbur, turning, saw the old scout saluting, and with stirring patriotism, saluted, too.

"And now," said the old hunter. "I'll get dinner."

"That you'll not," said Wilbur indignantly. "I guess this is my house, and you're to be my first guest."

CHAPTER VIII
DOWNING A GIANT LUMBERJACK

"I don't believe," said Wilbur the next morning as they rode along the trail that led to the nearest of his "lookout points," "that any king or emperor ever had as fine a palace as this one."

The comparison was a just one. Throughout the part of the forest in which they were riding the whole sensation was of being roofed in and enclosed, the roof itself being of shifting and glowing green, through which at infrequent intervals broad streams of living light poured in, gilding with a golden bronze the carpet of pine needles, while the purple brown shafts of the trunks of the mighty trees formed a colonnade illimitable.

"I reckon every kind of palace," replied the Ranger, "had some sort of a forest for a pattern. I took an artist through the Rockies one time, an' he showed me that every kind of buildin' that had ever been built, and every kind of trimmin's that had been devised had started as mere copies of trees an' leaves."

"Well," said Wilbur, his mind going back to a former exclamation of the old woodsman, "you said this was your house."

"My house it is," said Rifle-Eye, "an' if you wait a few minutes I'll show you the view from one of my windows."

For two hours the hunter and the boy had been riding up a sharp slope, in places getting off their horses so as to give them the benefit of as little unnecessary carrying as possible, constantly ascending on a great granite spur twenty miles wide, between the Kaweah and King's River canyons. Now, suddenly they emerged from the shadowy roof of the forest to the bare surface of a ridge of granite.

"There's the real world," said Rifle-Eye; "it ain't goin' to hurt your eyes to look at it, same as a city does, and your own little worryin's soon drop off in a place like this."

He turned his horse slightly to the left, where a small group of mountain balsam, growing in a cleft of the granite, made a spot of shadow upon the very precipice's brink. The boy looked around for a minute or two without speaking, then said softly: "How fine!"

Three thousand feet below, descending in bold faces of naked rugged rock, broken here and there by ledges whereon mighty pines found lodgment, lay the valley of King's River, a thin, winding gleam of green with the water a silver thread so fine as only to be seen at intervals. Here and there in the depths the bottom widened to a quarter of a mile, and there the sunlight, falling on the young grass, gave a brilliancy of green that was almost startling in contrast with the dark foliage of the pines.

"What do you call that rock?" asked the boy, pointing to a tall, pyramidal mass of granite, buttressed with rock masses but little less noble than the central peak, between each buttress a rift of snow, flecked here and there by the outline of a daring spruce clinging to the rock, apparently in defiance of all laws of gravity.

"That is called 'Grand Sentinel,'" said the hunter, "and if you will take out your glasses you will see that from here you can overlook miles and miles of country to the west. This is about as high as any place on the south fork of the King's River until it turns north where Bubbs Creek runs into it."

Wilbur took out from their case his field-glasses and scanned the horizon carefully as far as he could see, then snapping them back into the case, he turned to the hunter, saying:

"No fire in sight here!"

"All right," replied Rifle-Eye, "then we'll go on to the next point."

That whole day was a revelation to Wilbur of the beauty and of the size of that portion of the forest which it was his especial business to oversee. Here and there the Ranger made a short break from the direct line of the journey to take the boy down to some miner's cabin or Indian shack, so that, as he expressed it, "you c'n live in a world of friends. There ain't no man livin', son," he continued, "but what'll be the better of havin' a kind word some day, an' the more of them you give, the more you're likely to have."

Owing to these deviations from the direct trail, it was late when they returned to Wilbur's little camp. But not even the lateness of the hour, nor the boy's fatigue, could keep down his delight in his tent home. He was down at the corral quite a long time, and when he came back Rifle-Eye asked him where he had been. The boy flushed a little.

"I hadn't seen Kit all day," he said, "so I went down and had a little talk to her."

The Ranger smiled and said nothing but looked well pleased. In the meantime he had quickly prepared supper, and Wilbur started in and ate as though he would never stop. At last he leaned back and sighed aloud.

"That's the best dinner I ever ate," he said; "I never thought fish could taste so good."

But he jumped up again immediately and took the dishes down to the spring to wash them. He had just dipped the plates into the pool under the spring when the old woodsman stopped him.

"You don't ever want to do that," he said. "There ain't any manner of use in foulin' a stream that you'll want to use all the time. Little bits of food, washin' off the plates, will soon make that water bad if you let them run in there. An' not only is that bad for you, but ef you'll notice, it's the overflow from that little pool that runs down through the meadow."

"And it would spoil the drinking water for the horses," exclaimed Wilbur; "I hadn't thought of that. I'm awfully glad you're along, Rifle-Eye, for I should be making all sorts of mistakes."

Under the advice of his friend Wilbur washed up and put away the dishes and then settled down for the evening. He made up his day's report, and then thought he would write a long letter. But he had penned very, few sentences when he began to get quite sleepy and to nod over the paper. The Ranger noted it, and told him promptly to go to bed.

"I'll finish this letter first," said Wilbur.

A moment or two later he was again advised to turn in, and again Wilbur persisted that he would finish the letter first. There was a short pause.

"Son," said Rifle-Eye, "what do you suppose you are ridin' from point to point of the forest for?"

"To see if there's any sign of fire," said the boy.

"And you've got to look pretty closely through those glasses o' yours, don't you?"

The boy admitted that they were a little dazzling and that he had to look all he knew how.

"Then, if you make your eyes heavy and tired for the next mornin', you're robbin' the Service of what they got you for—your eyesight, ain't you? I ain't forcin' you, noways. I'm only showin' you what's the square thing."

Wilbur put forward his chin obstinately, then, thinking of the kindness he had received from the Ranger all the way through, and realizing that he was in the right, said:

"All right, Rifle-Eye, I'll turn in."

About half an hour later, just as the old woodsman stretched himself on his pile of boughs outside the tent, he heard the boy mutter:

"I hope I'll never have to live anywhere but here."

The following day and the next were similar in many ways to the first. Wilbur and the Ranger rode the various trails, the boy learning the landmarks by which he might make sure that he was going right, and making acquaintance with the few settlers who lived in his portion of the forest. On Sunday morning, however, the Ranger told the boy he must leave him to his own devices.

"I've put in several days with you gettin' you started," he said, "an' I reckon I'd better be goin' about some other business. There's a heap o' things doin' all the time, an' as it is I'm pressed to keep up. But I'll drop in every now an' again, an' you're allers welcome at headquarters."

"I hate to have you go, Rifle-Eye," the boy replied, "and you certainly have been mighty good to me. I'll try not to forget all the things you've told me, and I'll look forward to seeing you again before long."

"I'll come first chance I can," replied the hunter. "Take care of yourself."

"Good-by, Rifle-Eye," called the boy, "and I'll look for your coming back." He watched the old man until he was lost to sight and then waited until the sound of the horse's hoofs on the hillside had ceased. He found a lump in his throat as he turned away, but he went into the tent, and went over his reports to see if they read all right before the Supervisor arrived. Then, thinking that it was likely his chief would come about noon, he exerted himself trying to make up an extra good dinner. He caught some trout, and finding some lettuce growing in the little garden, got it ready for salad, and then mixed up the batter for some "flapjacks," as the old hunter had shown him how. He had everything ready to begin the cooking, and was writing letters when he heard his guest coming up the trail, and went out to meet him.

After Wilbur had made his reports and got dinner, for both of which he received a short commendation, the Supervisor broached the question of the timber trespass.

"Loyle," he said, "McGinnis and I have measured up the lumber stolen. There's about four and a half million feet. You were with us when we first located the trespass, and I want you to come with us to the mill."

"Very well, Mr. Merritt," answered the boy.

"I don't want you to do any talking at all, unless I ask you a question. Then answer carefully and in the fewest words you can. Don't tell me what you think. Say what you know. I'll do all the talking that will be necessary."

Wilbur thought to himself that the conversation probably would not be very long, but he said nothing.

"That is," continued the other as an afterthought, "McGinnis and I. I don't suppose he can be kept quiet."

Wilbur grinned.

"But he usually knows what he is talking about, I should think," he hazarded.

"He does—on lumber." Then, with one of the abrupt changes of topic, characteristic of the man, the Supervisor turned to the question of intended improvements in that part of the forest where Wilbur was to be. He showed himself to be aware that the lad's appointment as Guard was not merely a temporary affair, but a part of his training to fit himself for higher posts, and accordingly explained matters more fully than he would otherwise have done. Reaching the close of that subject he rose to go suddenly. He looked around the tent.

"Got everything you want?" he demanded.

"Yes, indeed, sir," the boy replied. "It's very comfortable here."

"Got a watch?"

"No, Mr. Merritt, not now."

"Why not?"

"Mine got lost in that little trouble I had with the bob-cat, and I didn't notice it until next day."

"Saw you hadn't one the other day. Take this."

He pulled a watch out of his pocket and handed it to the boy.

"But, Mr. Merritt," began the boy, "your watch? Oh, I couldn't — "

"Got another. You'll need it." He turned and walked out of the tent.

Wilbur overtook him on the way to the corral.

"Oh, Mr. Merritt — " he began, but his chief turned sharply round on him. The boy, for all his impulsiveness, could read a face, and he checked himself. "Thank you very much, indeed," he ended quietly. He got out the Supervisor's horse, and as the latter swung himself into the saddle, he said:

"What time to-morrow, Mr. Merritt?"

"Eleven, sharp," was the reply. "So long."

Wilbur looked after him as he rode away.

"That means starting by daybreak," he said aloud. "Well, I don't think I'm going to suffer from sleeping sickness on this job, anyway." And he went back into the tent to finish the letter which he had started two evenings before and never had a chance to complete.

By dawn the next morning Wilbur was on the trail. He was giving himself more time than he needed, but he had not the slightest intention of arriving late, neither did he wish the flanks of his horse to show that he had been riding hard. For the boy was perfectly sure that not a detail would escape the Supervisor's eye. Accordingly, he was able to take the trip quietly and trotted easily into camp a quarter of an hour ahead of time. He was heartily welcomed by McGinnis, while Merritt told him to go in and get a snack, as they would start in a few minutes. There was enough to make a good meal, and Wilbur was hungry after riding since dawn, so that he had just got through when the other two men rode up. He hastily finished his last mouthful, jumped up, and clambered into the saddle after the Supervisor, who had not waited a moment to see if he were ready.

Merritt set a fairly fast pace, and the trail was only intended for single file, so that there was no conversation for an hour or more. Then the head of the forest pulled up a little and conversed with McGinnis briefly for a while, resuming his rapid pace as soon as they were through. Once, and once only, did he speak to Wilbur, and that was just as they got on the road leading to the sawmill. There he said:

"Think all you like, but don't say it."

When they reached the mill they passed the time of day with several of the men, who seemed glad to see them, and a good deal of good-natured banter passed between McGinnis and the men to whom he was well known. The Supervisor sent word that he wanted to see the boss, and presently Peavey Jo came out to meet them.

"Salut, Merritt!" he said; "I t'ink it's long time since you were here, hey?"

The words as well as the look of the man told Wilbur his race and nation. Evidently of French origin, possibly with a trace of Indian in him, this burly son of generations of voyageurs looked his strength. Wilbur had gone up one winter to northern Wisconsin and Michigan where some of the big lumber camps were, and he knew the breed. He decided that Merritt's advice was extremely good; he would talk just as little as he had to.

The Supervisor wasted no time on preliminary greetings. That was not his way.

"How much lumber did you cut last winter off ground that didn't belong to you?" he queried shortly.

"Off land not mine?"

"You heard my question!"

"I cut him off my own land," said the millman with an injured expression.

"Some of it."

"You scale all the logs I cut. You mark him. I sell him. All right."

"You tell it well," commented the Supervisor tersely. "But it don't go, Jo. How much was there?"

"I tell you I cut him off my land."

Merritt pointedly took his notebook from his breastpocket.

"Liars make me tired," he announced impartially.

"You call me a liar—" began the big lumberman savagely, edging up to the horse.

"Not yet. But I probably will before I'm through," was the unperturbed reply.

"You say all the same that I am a liar, is it not?"

"Not yet, anyway. What does it matter? You cut four and a half million feet, a little over."

A smile passed over the faces of the men attached to the sawmill. It was evident that a number of them must know about the trespass, and probably thought that Peavey Jo had been clever in getting away with it. The mill-owner laughed.

"You t'ink I keep him in my pocket, hey?" he queried. "Four and a half million feet is big enough to see. You have a man here, he see logs, he mark logs, I cut them."

The Supervisor swung himself from his horse and handed the reins to Wilbur. McGinnis did the same.

"You don't need to get down, Loyle," he said; "it will not take long to find where the logs are."

The big lumberman stepped forward with an angry gleam in his eye.

"This my mill," he said. "You have not the right to walk it over."

"This is a National Forest," was the sharp reply, "and I'm in charge of it. I'll go just wherever I see fit. Who'll stop me?"

"Me, Josef La Blanc — I stop you."

Just then Wilbur, glancing over the circle of men, saw standing among them Ben, the half-witted boy who lived in the old hunter's cabin. Seeing that he was observed, the lad sidled over to Wilbur and said, in a low voice, questioningly:

"Plenty, plenty logs? No marked?"

"Yes," said Wilbur, wondering that he should have followed the discussion so closely.

"I know where!"

"You do?" queried Wilbur.

Ben nodded his head a great many times, until Wilbur thought it would fall off. In the meantime Merritt and Peavey Jo, standing a few feet apart, had been eying each other. Presently the Supervisor stepped forward:

"Show me those logs," he ordered.

"You better keep back, I t'ink," growled the millman.

Merritt stepped forward unconcernedly, but was met with an open-hand push that sent him reeling backward.

"I not want to fight you," he cried; "I get a plenty fight when I want him. You no good; can't fight."

"I'm not going to fight," said the Supervisor, "but I'm going to see where those logs are, or were. Stand aside!"

But the big Frenchman planted himself squarely in the way.

"If you hunt for the trouble," he said, "you get him sure," he said menacingly.

"I'm not hunting for trouble, Jo, and you know it But I'm hunting logs, and I'll find them."

He was just about to step forward, trusting to quickness to dodge the blow that he could see would be launched at him, when Ben, who had been whispering to Wilbur, lurched over to the Supervisor and pulled his arm.

"Plenty, plenty logs, no mark," he said loudly; "I know where. I show you. They are up—"

But he never finished the sentence, for the lumberman, taking one step forward, drove his left fist square at the side of the boy's jaw, dropping him insensible before he could give the information which Merritt was seeking.

But unexpected as the blow had been, it was met scarcely a second later by an equally unexpected pile-driver jolt from McGinnis.

"Ye big murdhering spalpeen," burst out the angry Irishman, "ye think it's a fine thing to try and shtop a man that's trying to do his duty, and think yerself a fightin' man, bekass ye can lick a man that doesn't want to fight. This isn't any Forest Service scrap, mind ye, and I'm saying nothing about logs. I'm talking about your hittin' a weak, half-crazed boy. Ye're a liar and a coward, Peavey Jo, and a dirty one at that."

"Keep quiet, McGinnis," said Merritt, who was stooping down over the insensible lad, "we'll put him in jail for this."

"Ye will, maybe," snorted the Irishman, "afther he laves the hospital."

"You make dis your bizness, hey?" queried the mill-owner.

"I'll make it your funeral, ye sneaking half-breed Canuck! How about it, boys," he added turning to the crowd, "do I get fair play?"

A chorus of "Sure," "'Twas a dirty trick," "The kid didn't know no better," and similar cries showed how the sentiment of the crowd lay. In a moment McGinnis and the Frenchman had stripped their coats and faced each other. The mill-owner was by far the bigger man, and the play of his shoulders showed that his fearful strength was not muscle bound, but he stood ponderously; on the other hand, the Irishman, who, while tall, was not nearly as heavy, only seemed to touch the ground, his step was so light and springy.

The Frenchman rushed, swinging as he did so. A less sure fighter would have given ground, thereby weakening the force of his return blow should he have a chance to give it. McGinnis sidestepped and cross-jolted with his left. It was a wicked punch, but Peavey Jo partly stopped it. As it was, it jarred him to his heels.

"Lam a kid, will ye, ye bloated pea-jammer," grinned McGinnis, who was beaming with delight now that the fight was really started.

"You fight, no talk," growled the other, recovering warily, for the one interchange had showed him that the Irishman was not to be despised.

"I can sing a tune," said McGinnis, "and then lick you with one hand — " He stopped as Peavey Jo bored in, fighting hard and straight and showing his mettle. There was no doubt of it, the Frenchman was the stronger and the better man. Twice McGinnis tried to dodge and duck, but Peavey Jo, for all his size, was lithe when roused and knew every trick of the trade, and a sigh went up when with a sweeping blow delivered on the point of the shoulder, the Frenchman sent McGinnis reeling to the ground. He would have kicked him with his spiked boots as he lay, in the fashion of the lumber camps, but the Supervisor, showing not the slightest fear of the infuriated giant, quietly stepped between.

"This fight's none of my making or my choosing," he said, "but I'll see that it's fought fair."

But before the bullying millman could turn his anger upon the self-appointed referee, McGinnis was up on his feet.

"Let me at him," he cried, "I'll show him a trick or two for that."

Again the fight changed color. McGinnis was not smiling, but neither had he lost his temper. His vigilance had doubled and his whole frame seemed to be of steel springs. Blow after blow came crashing straight for him, but the alert Irishman evaded them by the merest fraction of an inch. Two fearful swings from Peavey Jo followed each other in rapid succession, both of which McGinnis avoided by stepping inside them, his right arm apparently swinging idly by his side. Then suddenly, at a third swing, he ran in to meet it, stooped and brought up his right with all the force of arm and shoulder and with the full spring of the whole body upwards. It is a difficult blow to land, but deadly. It caught Peavey Jo on the point of the chin and he went down.

One of the mill hands hastened to the boss.

"You've killed him, I think," he said.

"Don't you belave it," said McGinnis; "he was born to be hanged, an' hanged he'll be."

But the big lumberman gave no sign of life.

"I have seen a man killed by that uppercut, though," said the Irishman a little more dubiously, as the minutes passed by and no sign of consciousness was apparent, "but I don't believe I've got the strength to do it."

Several moments passed and then Peavey Jo gave a deep respiration.

"There!" said McGinnis triumphantly. "I told ye he'd live to be hanged." He looked around for the appreciation of the spectators. "But it was a bird of a punch I handed him," he grinned.

CHAPTER IX
A HARD FOE TO CONQUER

With the defeat of Peavey Jo, and the evidence that he was not too seriously hurt by the licking he had received, the Supervisor's attention promptly returned to the question for which he had come to the mill. Ben had struggled up to a sitting posture, and Merritt repeated his question as to the whereabouts of the logs, the answering of which had brought the big millman's anger upon the half-witted lad. Accordingly, Ben looked frightened, and refused to answer, but when he saw his foe still lying stretched out on the ground he said:

"Logs, near, near. Under pile of slabs."

"Oh, that was the way he hid them," said the Forest Chief; "clever enough trick, too."

McGinnis and Merritt followed Ben, and a couple of the men around sauntered along also. Wilbur stayed with the horses, watching the mill-hands trying to bring Peavey Jo to consciousness. They had just roused him and got him to his feet when the government party returned.

"I've seen your logs," said the Supervisor with just a slight note of triumph in his voice, "and I've plenty of witnesses. I also know who you're working for, so it will do no good to skip out. I'll nail both of you. Four and a half million feet, remember."

Suddenly McGinnis startled every one by a sudden shout:

"Drop that ax!" he cried.

The lumberman, who was just about to get into the saddle, suddenly dropped from the stirrup and made a quick grab for Ben, who had been standing near by. The half-witted lad had picked up an ax, and was quietly sidling up in the direction of the lumberman, who was still too dazed from the blow he had received from McGinnis to be on the watch.

"What would ye do with the ax, ye little villain?" asked McGinnis.

"I kill him, once, twice," said the lad.

"Ye would, eh? Sure, I've always labored under the impression that killin' a man once is enough. 'Tis myself that can see the satisfaction it would be to whack him one with the ax, Ben, but ye'd be robbing the hangman."

"I kill him," repeated the half-witted lad.

"Not with that ax, anyway," said McGinnis wrenching it from his grasp and tossing it to one of the men who stood by. "I'm thinkin', Merritt, that we'd better take the boy away. When he's sot, there's no changin' him."

"You fellers had best take one o' my ponies," spoke up one of the sawyers; "I've got a string here, an' you can send him back any time. An' I guess it wouldn't be healthy here for Ben right now."

"All right, Phil," said McGinnis; "I'll go along with you and get him."

As soon as McGinnis was out of the way, Peavey Jo stepped up to where the Supervisor was sitting in the saddle. Ben had been standing beside him since McGinnis took the ax, but now he shrank back to Wilbur's side.

"You t'ink me beaten, hey?" he said, showing his teeth in an angry snarl; "you wait and see."

"I don't know whether you're beaten or no," said Merritt contemptuously, "but any one can see that you've been licked."

"You t'ink this forest good place. By Gar, I make him so bad you ashamed to live here."

"A threat's no more use than a lie, Peavey Jo," replied the Supervisor sharply. "I don't bluff worth a cent, and the government's behind me."

The half-breed spat on the ground.

"That for your American government," he said. "I, me, make your American government look sick. I warn you fairly now. You win this time, yes, but always, no. Bon! My turn come by and by."

"All right," replied the head of the forest indifferently, turning away as McGinnis and Ben came up, "turn on your viciousness whenever you like." Saying which, he rode away without paying further heed to the muttered response of the millman.

The ride home was singularly silent. Neither McGinnis nor the half-witted lad were in any mood for speaking, Ben nursing a badly swollen jaw, and McGinnis weak from the body blows and the lame shoulder he had received in the fight. The Supervisor was angry that the trouble had come to blows, but in justice could not blame McGinnis for the part he had taken. It annoyed him, especially, to feel that he had been compelled to take the part of a mere spectator, although this feeling was partly soothed by the knowledge that he had discovered and proved the very thing he had set out to find.

On arriving at headquarters, the four horses were turned into the corral, and the men went in to get supper. Merritt immediately commenced a full report to Washington on the case, and McGinnis and Ben were glad to lie down. At supper Wilbur took occasion to congratulate McGinnis on the result of the encounter. The Irishman nodded.

"He's a better man than me," he admitted readily, "and that uppercut was the only thing I had left. But 'tis a darlin' of a punch, is that same, when ye get it in right. But I don't think we're through with him. He looks like the breed that harbors a grudge."

"He threatened Merritt while you were away," said Wilbur, dropping his voice so as not to disturb the rest.

"The mischief he did! The nerve of him! Tell me what he said."

Wilbur repeated the conversation word for word, and the Irishman whistled.

"There, now," he said. "What did I tell ye? Not that I can see there's much that he can do."

"Do you suppose he'd set a fire?" asked Wilbur.

"He's mean enough to," said McGinnis, "but I don't believe he would. No man that knows anything at all about timber would. Sure, he knows that we could put it out in no time if there wasn't a wind, and if there was, why the blaze might veer at any minute and burn up his mill and all his lumber."

"But for revenge?"

"A Frenchy pea-jammer isn't goin' to lose any dollars unless he has to," said McGinnis. "I don't think you need to be afraid of that." Then, following along the train of thought that had been suggested, he told the boy some lurid stories of life in the lumber camps of Michigan and Wisconsin in the early days.

Early next morning Wilbur returned to his camp to resume his round of fire rides, which he found to be of growing interest. On his return to his camp, although tired, the lad would work till dark over his little garden, knowing that everything he succeeded in growing would add to the enrichment of his food supply. Then the fence around the garden was in very bad repair, and he set to work to make one which should effectively keep out the rabbits.

Another week he found that if he could build a little bridge across a place where the canyon was very narrow he could save an hour's ride on one of his trails. Already the lad had put up a small log span on his own account. He went over and over this line of travel, blazing his way until he felt entirely sure that he had picked out the best line of trail, and then one evening he called up Rifle-Eye and asked him if he would come over some time and show him how to build this little bridge.

There followed three most exciting days in which the Ranger and a Guard from the other side of the forest joined him in bridge-building. They not only spanned the canyon, but strengthened the little log bridge the boy had made all by himself. Wilbur's reward was not only the shortening of his route, but commendation from Rifle-Eye that he had taken the trouble to find out the route and that he had picked it so well. That night he wrote home as though he had been appointed in charge of all the forests of the world, so proud was he.

Then there was one day in which Wilbur found the value of his lookout, for from the very place that the old hunter had pointed out as being one of "the windows of his house," the boy saw curling up to the westward a small, dull cloud of smoke. Remembering the warnings of the Ranger, he did not leap to the saddle at once, but remained for several minutes, studying the nearest landmarks to the apparent location of the fire and the surest method of getting there. That ride was somewhat of a novel experience for Kit as well as the boy. The little mare had grown accustomed to a quiet, even pace on the forest trails, and the use of the spur was a thing not to be borne. Wilbur felt as if he were fairly flying through the pine woods. Still he remembered to keep the mare well in hand going down the steeper slopes, and within a couple of hours he found himself at the fire. Then Wilbur found how true it was that a blaze could easily be put out if caught early. There was little wind, and the line of fire was not more than a mile long. By clearing the ground, brushing the needles aside for a foot or so on the lee side of the fire, most of it burned itself out and the rest he could stamp to extinction. Here and there he used his fire shovel and threw a little earth where the blaze was highest.

That evening he telephoned to headquarters, reporting that he had put the fire out, but only received a kindly worded rebuke for not having endeavored to find out what caused the fire, and a suggestion that he should ride back the next day and investigate. But before he could telephone himself the next evening, and while he was at supper, the 'phone rang, and he found the Supervisor was on the wire.

"Come to headquarters at once," he was told; "all hands are wanted."

"To-night, Mr. Merritt?" the boy queried.

There was a moment's pause.

"What did you do to-day?" he asked in answer.

"I went to find out what started that fire," the boy replied. "It was a couple of fishermen from the city. They had been here before, and so had no guide. I followed them up and showed them how to make a fire properly."

"That's a pretty long ride," said Merritt; "I guess you can come over first thing to-morrow morning."

"Very well, sir," said Wilbur, and hung up the receiver.

"I certainly do wonder," he said aloud, "what it can be? It can't be a big fire, or he would tell me to come anyway, no matter what I'd done to-day, especially as fire is best fought at night. And I don't see how it can be any trouble over Peavey Jo, because that's in the hands of the Washington people now. Unless," he added as an afterthought, "they have come to arrest him."

Having settled in his mind that this was probably the trouble, Wilbur returned to his supper. Just as he was finishing it, he said aloud: "I don't see how it can be that, either. For if it's due to any trouble of that kind they want big, husky fellows, and Merritt can swear in any one he needs." So giving up the problem as temporarily insoluble, Wilbur went to bed early so as to make a quick start in the dawn of the morning.

It turned out to be a glorious day, with but very little wind, and Wilbur's mind was quite set at rest about the question of fire. But when he reached headquarters he was surprised to see the number of men that were gathered there. Not laughing and joking, as customarily, they stood gravely around, only eying him curiously as he came in. The boy turned to McGinnis.

"What's wrong?" he said.

For answer the lumberman held out a piece of wood from which the bark had been stripped. Underneath the bark on the soft wood were numberless little channels which looked as though they had been chiseled out with a fine, rounded chisel.

"Oh," he said, "I see." Then he continued: "But I didn't know there was any bark-beetle here."

McGinnis waved his hand around.

"Does this look as if we had known very long?" he said.

"Who found it out?" asked Wilbur.

"Rifle-Eye," was the reply, "or at least Merritt and he found traces on the same day and brought the news into camp. Merritt only saw signs in one spot, but the old Ranger dropped on several colonies at different parts of the forest, so that it must be widespread."

The boy whistled under his breath. He had heard enough of the ravages of the bark beetle to know what it might mean if it once secured a strong footing on the Sierras.

"I remember hearing once," he said, "that over twenty-two thousand acres of spruce in Bohemia were wiped out in a month by the Tomicus beetle."

"This is the work of a Tomicus," said McGinnis. "And what such a critter as that was ever made for gets me."

"What's going to be done?" asked Wilbur.

McGinnis pointed to the house whence the Supervisor was just coming out.

"I have notified the District Forester," he said, standing on the steps, "and if I find things in bad shape he will send for Wilcox, who knows more about the beetle than any man in the Service. I don't know how much damage has been done nor how widespread it is. There are eight of us here, and we will divide, as I said before, each two keeping about fifty yards apart and girdling infected and useless trees. Loyle, you go with Rifle-Eye."

Wilbur was delighted at finding himself with his old friend again, and he seized the opportunity gladly of asking him how he happened to find out that the pest had got a start.

"I was campin' last night," said the old Ranger, "an' I saw an old dead tree that looked as if it might have some tinder that would start a fire easy. So I picked up my ax an' went up to it. But the minute I got there I felt somethin' was wrong, so I sliced along the bark, an' there were hundreds of the beetles. Then I looked at some of the near by trees, an' there was a few, here and there. But the funny part of it was that although I looked, an' looked carefully, for a hundred yards on either side, I couldn't find any more."

"So much the better," said Wilbur, "you didn't want to find any more, did you?"

The old hunter stepped over to a spruce and examined it closely.

"I didn't think there were any there," he said, "but you can't be too sure."

They walked all the rest of the morning, without having seen a sign of any beetles, though once the most distant party whooped as a sign that some had been found.

"I remember," said the Ranger, "one year when we had a plague o' caterpillars. They was eatin' the needles of the trees an' killin' 'em by wholesale. There was nothin' we could do to stop it. But it got stopped all right."

"How?" Wilbur queried interestedly. "Rain?"

"Rain would only make it worse. Have you ever noticed, son, that when somethin' pretty bad comes along, there's always somethin' else comes to sort o' take off the smart? Nothin's bad all the time. Well, this time, there came a fly."

"A fly?"

"Yes, son, a fly, lookin' somethin' like a wasp, only not as long as your thumb-nail. They come in swarms, an' started disposin' o' them caterpillars as though they had been trained to the business. They stung 'em an' then dropped an egg where they'd stung. Sometimes the caterpillar lived long enough to spin a web, as they usually do, but it never come out as a moth. An' since it's the moth that lays the eggs, this fly put an end to the caterpillar output with pleasin' swiftness."

"What did they call the fly?"

"I did hear," said Rifle-Eye, thinking. "Oh, yes, now I remember; it was the ik, ik—"

"Oh, I know now," said Wilbur; "I remember hearing about it at the Ranger School. The ichneumon fly."

"That's it. But, as I was sayin'—" he stopped short. Then the old hunter took a quick step to one side, pointed at a pine tree, and said:

"There's one o' them."

Wilbur could only see a few little holes in the bark, but the old woodsman, slicing off a section, showed the tree girdled with the galleries that the beetle had made. He raised a whoop, and Wilbur in the distance could hear the Supervisor saying, "Three," implying it was the third piece found infected.

"But I don't quite see," said Wilbur, "how they make these galleries running in all sorts of ways."

"I ain't no expert on this here," said Rifle-Eye. "But as far as I know, in the spring a beetle finds an old decayed tree. She begins at once to bore a sort of passageway, half in the bark an' half in the wood, an' lays eggs all along the sides. When the eggs come out, each grub digs a tunnel out from the big gallery, an' in about three weeks the grub has made a long tunnel, livin' on the bark an' wood for its food, an' has grown to be a beetle. Then it bores its way out an' flies away to another tree to repeat the same interestin' performance."

"And if there are a lot of them," said Wilbur, "I suppose it stops the sap from going up."

"Exactly," said the hunter. "But they generally begin on sickly trees."

"Wilbur," he called a moment later, "come here."

The boy hurried over to the old hunter, who was standing by a dead tree — a small one, lying on the ground.

"Try that one," he said.

The boy struck it with the ax and it showed up alive with beetles and grubs and honeycombed with galleries.

"Gee," said the boy, "that's a bad one."

"That's very like the way I found the other," said the old hunter; "one very bad one lyin' on the ground an' just a few around it bad, while just a short distance away there was no signs."

He stood and thought for a minute or two, but aside from the coincidence, Wilbur could not see that there was anything strange in that. They worked busily for a few moments, girdling the infected trees, and also girdling some small useless trees near by, because, as the hunter explained, when the beetles flew out seeking a new tree to destroy, they would prefer one that was dying, as a tree from which all the bark has been cut away all round always does, and then these trees could be burned.

"Have you noticed wheel tracks around here?" asked the hunter thoughtfully.

"I did think so," said Wilbur, "near that dead tree, but I s'posed, of course, I was wrong. What would a wagon be doing up here?"

Suddenly the Ranger dropped his ax as though he had been stung. He turned to the boy, his eyes flashing.

"Boy!" he said, "did you see the stump of that dead tree!"

"I didn't notice," said Wilbur wonderingly.

The old woodsman picked up his ax, and led the way back to the dead tree.

Wilbur looked at the base of the tree.

"It isn't a windfall," he said; "it's been cut."

"Where's the stump?" asked Rifle-Eye.

The boy looked within a radius of a few feet, then looked up at the hunter.

"Where's the stump?" repeated the old man.

Wilbur turned back and searched for five minutes. Not a stump could he find that fitted the tree. None had been cut for some time, and none at all of so small a girth.

"I can't find any," he admitted shamefacedly, afraid that the Ranger would prove him wrong in some way.

"Nor can I," said Rifle-Eye. "Well?"

"Then I guess there isn't one there," said the boy.

"How did the tree get there?"

Wilbur looked at him, reflecting the question that he saw in the other's eyes.

"It couldn't get there of itself," he said, "and it was cut, too."

"An' wheel-tracks?"

"There were tracks," said the boy, "I'm sure of that."

"When a cut tree is found lyin' all by itself," said the Ranger, "with wagon tracks leadin' up to it an' away from it, it don't need a city detective to find out that some one dropped it there. An' when that dead tree is full of bark-beetle, an' there ain't none in the forest, that sure looks suspicious. An' when you find two of 'em jest the same way, with beetle in both, an' wheel-tracks near both, ye don't have to have a dog's nose to scent somethin's doin' that ain't over nice."

"But who," said Wilbur indignantly, "would do a trick like that?"

"The man that drove that wagon," said the old hunter. "I reckon, son, you an' me'll do a little trailin' an' see where those wheels lead us."

They left the place where the tree was lying and followed the faint mark of the wheels. In a few minutes they crossed the line of the Supervisor's inspection and he called to them.

"Hi, Rifle-Eye," he said, "you're away off the line."

"I know," said the old Ranger, "but I've got a plan of my own."

Merritt shrugged his shoulders, but he knew that Rifle-Eye never wasted his time, and he said no more. The old hunter and the boy walked on nearly a quarter of a mile, and there they found the tracks running beside a tiny gully, and a little distance down this, just as it had been thrown, was another of these small trees, equally filled with beetle.

"I don't think we'll find any stump to this one, either," said Wilbur gleefully, for he saw that they were on the right track.

"You will not," replied the other sternly. After they had girdled the infected trees again the Ranger shouldered his ax and, abandoning the tracks of the wheels, started straight for headquarters.

At supper all sorts of conjectures were expressed as to the cause of the pest, its extent, and similar matters, but Rifle-Eye said nothing. Wilbur was so full of the news that he was hardly able to eat anything for the information he was just bursting to give. But he kept it in. Finally, when the men had all finished and pipes were lighted, the old Ranger spoke, in his slow, drawling way, and every one stopped to listen.

"There's five of ye," he said, "that's found beetle, isn't there?"

"Yes," answered the Supervisor, "five."

"And I venture to bet," he continued, "that you found a dead tree lyin' in the middle of the infected patch!"

"Yes," said several voices, "we did."

"An' you didn't find much beetle except just round that one tree?"

"Not a bit," said one or two. "What about it?"

"There's a kind o' disease called Cholera," began Rifle-Eye in a conversational tone, "that drifts around a city in a queer sort o' way. It never hits two places at the same time, but if it goes up a street, it sort o' picks one side, an' stops at one place for a while then goes travelin' on. It acts jest as if a man was walkin' around, an' he was the cholera spirit himself."

"Well?" queried the Supervisor sharply.

The old Ranger smiled tolerantly at his impatience.

"Wa'al," he said, "I ain't believin' or disbelievin' the yarn. But I ain't believin' any such perambulatin' spirit for a bark-beetle. Especially when I finds wagon tracks leading to each place where the trouble is."

"What do you mean, Rifle-Eye?" asked Merritt. "Give it to us straight."

"I mean," he said, "that I ain't never heard of spirits needin' wagons to get around in. An' when I find dead trees containin' bark-beetles planted promiscuous where they'll do most good, I'm aimin' to draw a bead on the owner o' that wagon. An' I'll ask another thing. Did any o' you find the stumps of them infected trees?"

There was a long pause, and then McGinnis, always the first to see, laughed out loud ruefully.

"'Tis a black sorrow to me," he said, "that I didn't let Ben welt him wid the ax the other day. Somebody else will have to do it now."

"You mean," said the Supervisor, flaming, "that those trees were deliberately brought here to infect the forest, trees full of beetles?"

"Sure, 'tis as plain as the nose on your face," said McGinnis. "An' it's dubs we were not to see it ourselves."

"And it was—?"

"The bucko pea-jammer that I gave a lickin' to in the spring, for sure," said McGinnis. "Peavey Jo, of course, who else?"

CHAPTER X

A FOURTH OF JULY PERIL

Wilbur stayed but a few days at headquarters, the Supervisor and Rifle-Eye having succeeded in trailing the wagon that had deposited the trees from the point of its entrance into the forest to the place it went out, by this means ensuring the discovery of all the spots where diseased trees had been placed. One of them was in Wilbur's section of the forest, and he was required to go weekly and examine all the trees in the vicinity of the infected spot to make sure that the danger was over. But, thanks to Rifle-Eye's discovery, the threatened pest was speedily held down to narrow limits.

This added not a little to the lad's riding, for the place where Peavey Jo had deposited the infected tree in his particular part of the forest was a long way from the trail to the several lookout points to which he went daily to watch for fires. Fortunately, having built the little bridge across the canyon, and thus on one of the days of the week having shortened his ride, he was able to use the rest of the day looking after bark-beetles. But it made a very full week. He could not neglect any part of these rides, for June was drawing to an end and there had been no rain for weeks.

One night, returning from a hard day, on which he had not only ridden his fire patrol, but had also spent a couple of hours rolling big rocks into a creek to keep it from washing out a trail should a freshet come, he found a large party of people at his camp. There was an ex-professor of social science of the old régime, his wife and little daughter, a guide, and a lavish outfit. Although the gate of Wilbur's corral was padlocked and had "Property of the U. S. Forest Service" painted on it, the professor had ordered the guide to smash the gate and let the animals in.

Wilbur was angry, and took no pains to conceal it.

"Who turned those horses into my corral?" he demanded.

The professor, who wore gold-rimmed eyeglasses above a very dirty and tired face, replied:

"I am in charge of this party, and it was done at my orders."

"By what right do you steal my pasture?" asked the boy hotly.

"I understood," said the professor loftily, "that it was the custom of the West to be hospitable. But you are probably too young to know. Your parents live here?"

"No," replied the lad. "I am a Forest Guard, and in charge of this station. You will have to camp elsewhere."

At these last words the flap of the tent was parted and a woman came out, the professor's wife, in fact. She looked very tired and much troubled.

"What is this?" she asked querulously. "Have we got to start again to-night?"

Wilbur took off his hat.

"I beg your pardon," he said, "I did not know there were ladies in the party." He turned to the professor. "I suppose if it will bother them I'll have to let you stay. But if it hadn't been for that I'd have turned every beast you've got out into the forest and let them rustle for themselves."

"Yes, you would!" said the guide. "An' what would I have had to say?"

"Nothing," said Wilbur, "except that I'd have you arrested for touching U. S. property." He turned to the professor: "How did you get here?" he said.

"Up that road," said the older man, pointing to the southwest.

"And why didn't you camp a couple of miles down? There's much better ground down there."

"The guide said there was no place at all, and he didn't know anything about this camp, either, and we thought we would have to go on all night."

Wilbur snorted.

"Guide!" he said contemptuously. "Acts more like a stable hand!"

"Well," said the professor testily, "if there's been any damage done you can tell your superiors to send me a bill and I'll take the matter up in Washington. In the meantime, we will stay here, and if I like it here, I will stay a week or two."

"Not much, you won't," said Wilbur, "at least you won't have any horses in the corral after daybreak to-morrow morning. I'll let them have one good feed, anyhow, and if they're traveling with a thing like that to look after them," — he pointed to the "guide," — "they'll need a rest. But out they go to-morrow."

"We will see to-morrow," said the camper.

"In the meantime, I see a string of trout hanging there. Are they fresh?"

"I caught them early this morning," answered Wilbur, "before I began my day's work."

The professor took out a roll of bills.

"How much do you want for them!" he asked.

"They are not for sale," the boy replied.

"Oh, but I must have them," the other persisted. "I had quite made up my mind to have those for supper to-night."

"And I suppose, if I hadn't come home when I did," said Wilbur, "you would have stolen those, too!"

"I would have recompensed you adequately," the former college official replied. "And you have no right to use the word 'stolen.' I shall report you for impertinence."

By this time Wilbur was almost too angry to talk, and, thinking it better not to say too much, he turned on his heel and went to his own tent. Before going down to the corral with Kit, however, he took the precaution of carrying the string of fish with him, for he realized that although the professor would not for the world have taken them without paying, he would not hesitate to appropriate them in his absence. He cooked his trout with a distinct delight in the thought that the intruders had nothing except canned goods.

In the morning Wilbur was up and had breakfast over before the other camp was stirring. As soon as the "guide" appeared Wilbur walked over to him.

"I've given you a chance to look after your animals," he said, "before turning them out. You take them out in ten minutes or I'll turn them loose."

"Aw, go on," said the other, "I've got to rustle grub. You haven't got the nerve to monkey with our horses."

Promptly at the end of the ten minutes Wilbur went over to the "guide" again.

"Out they go," he said.

But the other paid no attention. Wilbur went down to the corral, the gate of which he had fixed early that morning, caught his own two mounts, and tied them. Then he opened the gate of the corral and drove the other eight horses to the gate. In a moment he heard a wild shout and saw the "guide" coming down the trail in hot haste. He reached the corral in time to head off the first of his horses which was just coming through. Wilbur had no special desire to cause the animals to stray, and was only too well satisfied to help the "guide" catch them and tie up to trees about the camp. By this time it was long after the hour that the boy usually began his patrol, but he waited to see the party start. As they were packing he noticed a lot of sticks that looked like rockets.

"What are those?" he asked. "If they're heavy, you're putting that pack on all wrong."

"These ain't got no weight," said the "guide"; "that's just some fireworks for the Fourth. We've got a bunch of them along for the little girl. She's crazy about fireworks."

Wilbur said no more, but waited until the professor came out. Then he walked up to him.

"I understand," he said, "that you have some fireworks for the Fourth."

The man addressed made no reply, but walked along as though he had not heard.

"I give you fair warning," said Wilbur, "that you can't set those off in this forest, Independence Day or no Independence Day."

"We shan't ask your permission," said the old pedant loftily. "In fact, some will be set off this evening, and some to-morrow, wherever we may be."

"But don't you understand," the boy said, "that you're putting the forest in danger, in awful danger of fire? And if a big forest fire starts, you are just as likely to suffer as any one else. You might cause a loss of millions of dollars for the sake of a few rockets."

"The man that sold me them," said the other, "said they were harmless, and he ought to know."

"All right," said Wilbur. "I've been told off to protect this forest from danger of fire, and if there's any greater danger around than a bunch like yours I haven't seen it. I reckon I'll camp on your trail till you're out of my end of the forest, and then I'll pass the word along and see that there's some one with you to keep you from making fools of yourselves."

He turned on his heel and commenced to make up a pack for his heavier horse, intending to ride Kit. He then went to the telephone and, finding no one at headquarters, called up the old hunter's cabin. The Ranger had a 'phone put in for Ben, who had learned how to use it, and by good fortune the half-witted lad knew where to find Rifle-Eye. He explained to Ben how matters stood, and asked him to get word to the Ranger if possible. Then Wilbur went back to the party and gave them a hand to get started.

Although he had been made very angry, Wilbur could see no gain in sulking and he spent the day trying to establish a friendly relation with the professor, so that, as he expressed it afterwards, "he could jolly him out of the fireworks idea." But while this scholastic visitor was willing to talk about subjects in connection with the government, and was quite well-informed on reclamation projects, Wilbur found the professor as stubborn as a mule, and every time he tried to bring the conversation round to forest fires he would be snubbed promptly.

That evening Wilbur led the party to a camping place where, he reasoned, there would be little likelihood of fire trouble, as it was a very open stand and all the brush on it had been piled and burned in the spring. But the lad was at his wits' end what further to do. He could not seize and carry off all the fireworks, and even if he were able to do so, he couldn't see that he had any right to. It was a great relief to the boy when he heard a horse on the trail and the old Ranger cantered up.

"Oh, Rifle-Eye," he said, "I'm so glad you've come. Tell me what to do," and the boy recounted his difficulty with the party from first to last.

The old woodsman listened attentively, and then said:

"I reckon, son, we'll stroll over and sorter see just how the land lies. There's a lot of things can be done with a mule by talkin' to him, although there is some that ain't wholly convinced by a stick of dynamite. We'll see which-all these here are."

"I think they're the dynamite kind," the boy replied.

"Well, we'll see," the Ranger repeated. He stepped in his loose-jointed way to where the party was sitting around the campfire. Then, looking straight at the man of the party, he said:

"You're a professor?"

The remark admitted of no reply but:

"I was for twenty years."

"And what did you profess?"

At this the camper rose to his feet, finding it uncomfortable to sit and look up at the tall, gaunt mountaineer. He replied testily that it wasn't anything to do with Rifle-Eye what chair he had held or in what college, and he'd trouble him to go about his business.

Rifle-Eye heard him patiently to the end, and then asked again, without any change of voice:

"And what did you profess?"

Once again the reputed educator expressed himself as to the Ranger's interference and declared that he had been more annoyed since coming into the forest than if he had stayed out of it. He worked himself up into a towering rage. Presently Rifle-Eye replied quietly:

"You refuse to tell?"

117

"I do," snapped the professor.

"Is it because you are ashamed of what you taught, or of where you taught it?" the Ranger asked.

This was touching the stranger in a tender place. He was proud of his college and of his hobby, and he retorted immediately:

"Ashamed? Certainly not. I was Professor of Social Economy in Blurtville University."

"And what do you call Social Economy?" asked Rifle-Eye.

The educator fell into the trap thus laid out for him and launched into a vigorous description of his own peculiar personal views toward securing a better understanding of the rights of the poor and of modern plans for ensuring better conditions of life, until he painted a picture of his science and his own aims which was most admirable. When he drew breath, he seemed quite pleased with himself.

The Ranger thought a minute.

"An' under which of these departments," he said, "would you put breakin' into this young fellow's corral, and havin' your eight horses eatin' up feed which will hardly be enough for his two when the dry weather comes?"

"That's another matter entirely," replied the professor, becoming angry as soon as he was criticised.

"Yes, it's another matter," said Rifle-Eye. "It's doin' instead of talkin'. I reckon you're one o' the talkin' kind, so deafened by the sound o' your own splutterin' that you can't hear any one else. It's a pity, too, that you don't learn somethin' yourself before you set others to learnin'."

"Are you trying to teach me?" snapped the traveler.

The old Ranger leaned his arm on the barrel of his rifle, which, according to his invariable custom, he was carrying with him, a habit from old hunting days, and looking straight at the professor, said:

"I ain't no great shakes on Social Economy, as you call it, and I ain't been to college. But I c'n see right enough that there's no real meanin' to you in all

118

you know about the rich an' the poor when you'll go an' rob a lad o' the pasture he'll need for his horses; an' you're only actin' hypocrite in lecturin' about promotin' good feelin's in society when you're busy provokin' bad feelin' yourself. An' when you're harpin' on the deep canyon that lies between Knowledge an' Ignorance, it don't pay to forget that Politeness is a mighty easy bridge to rear, an' one that's always safe. You may profess well enough, Mister Professor, but you're a pretty ornery example o' practisin'."

"But it's none of your business—" interrupted the stranger angrily.

Rifle-Eye with a gesture stopped him.

"It's just as much my business to talk to you," he said, "as it'd be yours to talk to me. In fact it's more. You c'n talk in your lecture room, an' I'll talk here. Perhaps it ain't altogether your fault; it's just that you don't know any better. You're just a plumb ignorant critter out here, Mister Professor, an' by rights you oughtn't to be around loose.

"An' you tried to threaten a boy here who was doin' his duty by sayin' that you'd write to Washington. What for? Are you so proud o' thievin' an' bullyin' that you want every one to know, or do you want to tell only a part o' the story so as you'll look all right an' the other fellow all wrong. That breed o' Social Economy don't go, not out here. We calls it lyin', an' pretty mean lyin' at that."

He broke off suddenly and looked down with a smile.

"Well, Pussy," he said, "that's right. You come an' back me up," and reaching out his brown gnarled hand he drew to his side the little girl who had come trustingly forward to him as all children did, and now had slipped her little hand into his.

"An' then there's this question o' fire," he continued. "Haven't you got some fireworks for the Fourth, Pussy?" he said, looking down at his little companion.

"Oh, yeth," she lisped, "pin-wheelth, and crackerth, and thnaketh, and heapth of thingth."

"What a time we'll have," he said. "Shall we look at them now?"

"Oh, yeth," the little girl replied, and ran across to her father, "can we thee them now?"

"No, not now," the father replied.

The old Ranger called the "guide" by name.

"Miguel," he said, "the fireworks are wanted to-night. Bring 'em to me."

The professor protested, but a glance at the sinewy frame of the mountaineer decided Miguel, and he brought several packages. In order to please the little girl, Rifle-Eye lent her his huge pocket-knife and let her open the packages, sharing the surprises with her. Some of them he put aside, especially the rockets, but by far the larger number he let the child make up into a pile.

"Will you give me your word you won't set off these?" queried the mountaineer, pointing to the smaller pile of dangerous explosives with his foot.

"I'll say nothing," said the professor.

Without another word the Ranger stooped down, picked them up in one big armful, and disappeared beyond the circle of the light of the campfire into the darkness. He reappeared in a few minutes.

"I'm afeard," he said, "your fireworks may be a little wet. I tied 'em in a bundle, fastened a stone to 'em, an' then dropped 'em in that little lake. You can't do any harm with those you've got now." He waited a moment. "You can get those rockets," he said, "any time you have a mind to. That lake dries up about the middle of September."

"By what right—" began the professor.

"I plumb forget what sub-section you called that partickler right just now," Rifle-Eye replied, "but out here we calls it fool-hobblin'. You're off your range, Mister Professor, an' the change o' feed has got you locoed mighty bad. I reckon you'd better trot back to your own pastures in the East, an' stay there till you know a little more."

"What is your name and address?" blustered the professor; "I'll have the law invoked for this."

"There's few in the Rockies as don't know old Rifle-Eye Bill," the Ranger replied, "an' my address is wherever I c'n find some good to be done. Any one c'n find me when I'm wanted, an' I'm ready any time you say. Now, you're goin' to celebrate the Fourth to-morrow, to show how fond you are o' good government. You c'n add to your lectures on Social Economy one rule you don't know any thin' about. It's a Western rule, this one, an' it's just that no man that can't govern himself can govern anythin' else."

He turned on his heel, ignoring the reply shouted after him, and followed by Wilbur, mounted and rode away up the trail.

"I've got to get right back," said the Ranger; "we're goin' to start workin' out a special sale of poles."

"Telegraph poles?" queried Wilbur.

"Yes."

"When you come to think of it," said the boy, "there must be quite a lot of poles all over the country."

"Merritt said he reckoned there was about sixteen million poles now in use, an' three and a half million poles are needed every year just for telegraph and telephone purposes alone."

"When you think," said Wilbur, "that every telegraph and telephone pole means a whole tree, there's some forest been cut down, hasn't there?"

"How many poles do you s'pose are used in a mile?"

"About forty, I heard at school," the boy replied, "and it takes an army of men working all the year round just puttin' in poles."

The old hunter struck a match and put a light to his pipe.

"More forest destruction," said the boy mischievously, "I should think, Rifle-Eye, you'd be ashamed to waste wood by burning it up in the form of matches."

"Go on talkin'," said Rifle-Eye, "you like tellin' me these things you picked up at the Ranger School. Can you tell how much timber is used, or how many matches are lighted an' thrown away?"

"Three million matches a minute, every minute of the twenty-four hours," said Wilbur immediately. "That is," he added after a moment's calculation, "nearly four and a half billion a day. And then only the very best portion of the finest wood can be used, and, as I hear, the big match factories turn out huge quantities of other stuff, like doors and window sashes, in order to use up the wood which is not of the very finest quality, such as is needed for matches."

"How do they saw 'em so thin, I wonder?" interposed the Ranger.

"Some of it is sawed both ways," the boy replied. "Some logs are boiled and then revolved on a lathe which makes a continuous shaving the thickness of a match, and a lot of matches are paper-pulp, which is really wood after all. There's no saying, Rifle-Eye," he continued, laughing, "how many good trees have been cut down to make a light for your pipe."

The old hunter puffed hard, as the pipe was not well lighted.

"Well," he said, "I guess I'll let the Forest Guards handle it." He looked across at the boy. "It's up to you," he said, "to keep me goin.' Got a match?"

CHAPTER XI
AMIDST A CATTLE STAMPEDE

Wilbur would have liked greatly to be able to stay at his little tent home and celebrate the Fourth of July in some quiet fashion, but the fireworks folly of the professor's party had got on his nerve a little, and he was not satisfied until he really got into the saddle and was on his way to a lookout point. Nor was he entirely without reward, for shortly before noon, as he rode along his accustomed trail, a half-Indian miner met him and told him he had been waiting to ask him to dinner. And there, with all the ceremony the little shack could muster, this simple family had prepared a feast to the only representative of the United States that lived near them, and Wilbur, boy-like, had to make a speech, and rode along the trail later in the afternoon, feeling that he had indeed had a glorious Fourth of July dinner in the Indian's cabin.

The week following the Supervisor rode up, much to Wilbur's surprise, who had not expected to see him back in that part of the forest so soon. But Merritt, who indeed was anxious to get away, by his conversation showed that he was awaiting the arrival and conveyance of a trainload of machinery for the establishment of a large pulp-mill on the Kern River. The trail over which this machinery would have to be taken was brushed out and ready, all save about nine miles of it, a section too small to make it worth while to call a Ranger from another part of the forest. So the Supervisor announced his intention of doing the work himself, together with Wilbur. The night preceding, just before they turned in for the night, the boy turned to his chief and said:

"What time in the morning, Mr. Merritt?"

"I'll call you," replied the Supervisor.

He did, too, for at sharp five o'clock the next morning Wilbur was wakened to find the older man up and with breakfast ready.

"I ought to have got breakfast, sir," said the boy; "why didn't you leave it for me?"

"You need more sleep than I do," was the sufficient answer. "Now, tuck in."

The boy waited for no second invitation and devoted his attention to securing as much grub as he could in the shortest possible time. Breakfast was over, the camp straightened up, and they were in the saddle by a quarter to six. It was ten miles from Wilbur's camp to the point where the trail should start. The country was very rough, and it was drawing on for nine o'clock when they reached the point desired.

"Now," said the Supervisor, "take the brush hook and clear the trail as I locate it."

Wilbur, accordingly, following immediately after his chief, worked for all he knew how, cutting down the brushwood and preparing the trail. Every once in a while Merritt, who had blazed the trail some distance ahead, would return, and, bidding the boy pile brush, would attack the underwood as though it were a personal enemy of his and would cover the ground in a way that would make Wilbur's most strenuous moments seem trifling in comparison. Once he returned and saw the lad laboring for dear life, breathing hard, and showing by his very pose that he was tiring rapidly, although it was not yet noon, and he called to him.

"Loyle," he said, "what are you breaking your neck at it that way for?"

"I don't come near doing as much as I ought unless I do hurry," he said. "And then I'm a long way behind."

"You mean as much as me?"

The boy nodded.

"Absurd. No two men's speed is the same. Don't force work. Find out what gait you can keep up all day and do that. Make your own standard, don't take another man's."

"But I go so slowly!"

"Want to know it all and do it all the first summer, don't you? Suppose no one else had to learn? I don't work as hard as you do, though I get more done. You can't buck up against an old axman. I haven't done this for some time, but I guess I haven't forgotten how. Go and sit down and get your breath."

"But I'm not tired—" began Wilbur protestingly.

"Sit down," he was ordered, and the boy, feeling it was better to do what he was told, did so. After he had a rest, which indeed was very welcome, the Supervisor called him.

"Loyle," he said, "you know something about a horse, for I've watched you with them. Handle yourself the same way. You wouldn't force a horse; don't force yourself."

Moreover, the older man showed the boy many ways wherein to save labor, explaining that there was a right way and a wrong way of attacking every different kind of bush. In consequence, when Wilbur started again in the afternoon he found himself able to do almost half as much again with less labor. Working steadily all day until sundown, five miles of the trail had been located, brushed out, and marked.

There was a small lake near by, and thinking that it would be less fatiguing for the boy to catch fish than to look after the camp, the Supervisor sent him off to try his luck. Wilbur, delighted to have been lucky, returned in less than fifteen minutes with four middling-sized trout, and he found himself hungry enough to eat his two, almost bones and all. That night they slept under a small Baker tent that Merritt had brought along on his pack horse, the riding and pack saddles being piled beside the tent and covered with a slicker.

The following day, by starting work a little after daybreak, the remaining four miles of the trail were finished before the noonday halt, which was made late in order to allow the completion of the work. Wilbur, when he reviewed the fact that they had gone foot by foot over nine miles of trail, clearing out the brush and piling it, so that it could be burned and rendered harmless as soon as it was dry, thought it represented as big a two days' work as he had ever covered.

"Will the pulp-mill be above or below the new Edison plant?" queried Wilbur on their way home.

"Above," said his companion. "I'll show you just where. You're going to ride down with me to the site of the mill to-morrow. There's a lot of spruce here, and it ought to pay."

"But I thought," said Wilbur, "that paper-pulp was such a destructive way of using timber?"

"It is," answered Merritt, "but paper is a necessity. A book is more important than a board."

"But doesn't it take a lot of wood to make a little paper?" asked the boy. "There's been such a howl about paper-pulp that I thought it must be fearfully wasteful."

"It isn't wasteful at all," was the reply. "A cord and a half of spruce will make a ton of pulp. Where the outcry comes in is the quantity used. One newspaper uses a hundred and fifty tons of paper a day. That means two hundred and twenty-five cords of wood. The stand of spruce here is about ten cords to the acre. So one newspaper would clean off ten acres a day or three thousand acres a year."

"But wouldn't it ruin the forest to take it off at that rate?"

"Certainly," the Supervisor answered, "but the sale will be so arranged that not more will be sold each year than will be good for the forest."

"Is all paper made of spruce?" asked Wilbur.

"No. Many kinds of wood will make paper. Carolina poplar and tulip wood are both satisfactory."

"Except for the branches and knot-wood," said Wilbur, "almost every part of every kind of tree is good for something."

"And you can use those, too," came the instant reply. "That's what dry distillation is for. All that you've got to do is fill a retort with wood and put a furnace under it, and all pine tree leavings can be transformed into tar and acetic acid, from which they can make vinegar, as well as wood alcohol and charcoal."

Finding that the boy was thoroughly interested in the possibilities of lumber, the Supervisor, usually so silent and brief in manner, opened out a little and talked for two straight hours to Wilbur on the possibilities of forestry. He showed the value of turpentine and resin in the pine trees and advocated the planting of hemlock trees and oak trees for their bark, as used in the tanning industry.

As the Forester warmed up to his subject, Wilbur thought he was listening to an "Arabian Nights" fairy tale. Despite his customary silence Merritt was an enthusiast, and believed that forestry was the "chief end of man." He assured the boy that twenty different species of tree of immense value could be acclimatized in North America which are of great commercial value now in South America; he compared the climate in the valleys of the lower Mississippi with those of the Ganges, and named tree after tree, most of them entirely unknown to Wilbur, which would be of high value in the warm, swampy bottoms. And when Wilbur ventured to express doubt, he was confronted with the example of the eucalyptus, commonly called gum tree, once a native of Australia, now becoming an important American tree.

All the way home and all through supper the Supervisor talked, until when it finally became time to turn in, the boy dreamed of an ideal time when every acre of land in the United States should be rightly occupied; the arid land irrigated from streams fed by reservoirs in the forested mountains; the rivers full of navigation and never suffering floods; the farms possessing their wood-lots all duly tended; and every inch of the hills and mountains clothed with forests—pure stands, or mixed stands, as might best suit the conditions—each forest being the best possible for its climate and its altitude.

But he had to get up at five o'clock next morning, just the same, and dreams became grim realities when he found himself in the saddle again and off for a day's work before six. A heavy thunderstorm in the night had made everything fresh and shining, but at the same time the water on the underbrush soaked Wilbur through and through when he went out to wrangle the horses. Merritt's riding horse, a fine bay with a blazed face, had a bad reputation in the country, which Wilbur had heard, and he was in an ugly frame of mind when the boy found him. But Wilbur was not afraid of horses, and he soon got him saddled.

"I think Baldy's a little restless this morning, sir," ventured Wilbur, as they went to the corral to get their horses. But he received no answer. The Supervisor's fluent streak had worn itself out the day before and he was more silent than ever this morning.

Merritt swung himself into his saddle, and, as Wilbur expected, the bay began to buck. It was then, more than ever, that the boy realized the difference between the riding he had seen on the plains and ordinary riding. Merritt was a good rider, and he stuck to his saddle well. But Wilbur could see that it was with difficulty, and that the task was a hard one. There was none of the easy grace with which Bob-Cat Bob had ridden, and when Baldy did settle down Wilbur felt that his rider had considered his keeping his seat quite a feat, not regarding it as a trifling and unimportant incident in the day.

Merritt and the boy rode on entirely off the part of the forest on which Wilbur had his patrol, to a section he did not know. They stopped once to look over a young pine plantation. Just over a high ridge there was a wider valley traversed by an old road which crossed the main range about five miles west and went down into a valley where there were numerous ranches. The principal occupation of these ranchmen was stock-raising, on account of their long distance from a railroad which prevented them marketing any produce. Just about July of each year these ranchmen rounded up their stock, cut out the beef steers, and shipped them to the markets. It was then the last week in July, and the Supervisor expected to meet some of the herds upon the old road which crossed the mountains further on. Just as they reached the bottom of the hill they saw the leaders of a big herd coming down the road from the pass. In the distance a couple of cowpunchers could be seen in front holding up the lead of the bunch.

"I'll wait and talk," said Merritt, reining in. As perhaps he had exchanged four whole sentences in two hours' ride, Wilbur thought to himself that the conversation would have to be rather one-sided, but he knew the other believed in seizing every opportunity to promote friendliness with the people in his forest and waited their upcoming with interest. The Supervisor had his pack-horse with him, and as the herd drew nearer he told Wilbur to take him out of sight into the brush, so as not to scare the steers, and tie him up safely. That done, Wilbur rode back to the road.

By the time he had returned the two punchers had ridden up. One proved to be the foreman of the outfit, by name Billy Grier, and the other a Texan, whom Merritt called Tubby Rodgers, apparently because he was as thin as a lath.

"I was a-hopin'," said Grier as he rode up, "that you-all was headin' down the road a bit."

"I wasn't planning to," said the Forester. "Why?"

"We had a heavy storm down in the valley last night, which sort of broke things up badly, an' I had to leave a couple of men behind."

"Don't want to hire us to drive, do you?" asked Merritt.

"Allers willin' to pay a good man," said the foreman with a grin. "Give ye forty and chuck."

The Supervisor smiled.

"I'm supposed to be holding down a soft job," he said; "government service."

"Soft job," snorted Grier, "they'd have to give me the bloomin' forest afore I'd go at it the way you do. But, Merritt," he added, "this is how. A piece down the road, say a mile an' a half, I'm told there's a rotten bit o' road, an' I'm a little leery of trouble there. I'd have strung out the cattle three times as far if I'd known of it. But I had no chance; I've only just heard that some old county board is tryin' to fix a bridge, an' they're movin' about as rapid as a spavined mule with three broken legs."

"Well?" queried Merritt; "I suppose you want us to help you over that spot."

"That's it, pard," said the foreman; "an' I'll do as much for you some time."

"I wish you could, but I'll never have a string of cattle like those to turn into good hard coin."

"Well," said the cowpuncher, "why not?"

"Nothing doing," replied Merritt; "the Forest Service is an incurable disease that nobody ever wants to be cured of."

By this time the head of the bunch of steers was drawing close and the foreman repeated his request.

"All right," answered the Forester, who thought it good policy to have the ranchman feel that he was under obligations to the Service, "we'll give you a hand all right."

After riding down the road for about a mile it became precipitous, and Wilbur could readily see where there was likely to be trouble. Shortly before they reached the place where the bridge was being repaired the bank on the right-hand side of the road gave place to a sheer drop forty to fifty feet high and deepening with every step forward. As the bunch neared the bridge Merritt and Wilbur, with the cowpunchers, slowed up until the steers were quite close. Then Grier and Rodgers went ahead over the bridge, while Merritt waited until about fifty cattle had passed and then swung in among them, telling Wilbur to do the same when about another fifty head had passed.

At first Wilbur could not see the purpose of this, and he had great difficulty in forcing his horse among the cattle. But they pressed back as he swung into the road, giving him a little space to ride in, and thus dividing the head of the drove into two groups of fifty. Following instructions, Wilbur gradually pressed the pace of the bunch in order to prevent any chance of overcrowding from the rear.

It seemed easy enough. Owing to the narrowness of the road and the precipitous slope it was impossible for the steers to scatter, and as long as the pace was kept up, there was likely to be no difficulty. But Kit—Wilbur was riding Kit—suddenly pricked her ears and began to dance a little in her steps. The steers, although their pace had not changed, were snuffling in an uncertain fashion, and Wilbur vaguely became conscious that fear was abroad. He quieted Kit, but could see from every motion that she was catching the infection of the fear. He tightened his hold on the lines, for he saw that if she tried to bolt both of them would go over the edge. Wilbur looked down.

A hundred yards or so further on the road widened slightly, and Wilbur wondered whether it would be possible for him to work his way to the right of the steers and gallop full speed alongside the herd to get in front of them; but even as he thought of the plan he realized that it would scarcely be possible, and that unless he reached the front of the herd before the road narrowed again he would be forced over the edge. And, as he reached the wider place, he saw Grier and Rodgers standing. They also had sensed the notion of fear and were waiting to see what could be done in the main body of the herd. Merritt had worked his way through the steers, and was riding in the lead. Wilbur wondered how he had ever been able to force Baldy through. This put Wilbur behind a bunch of about one hundred steers and in front of five or six hundred more.

Below him, to the right, was a valley, the drop now being about one hundred and fifty feet, and Wilbur could see at the edge of the creek, pitched among some willows, a little tent, the white contrasting strongly with the green of the willows. The road wound round high above the valley in order to keep the grade. Twice Wilbur halted Kit to try to stop the foremost of the herd behind him from pressing on too close, but the third time Kit would not halt. She was stepping as though on springs, with every muscle and sinew tense, and the distance between the steers before and the steers behind was gradually lessening.

Wilbur realized that as long as the even, slow pace was kept he was in no danger, but if once the steers began to run his peril would be extreme. He could turn neither to the right nor to the left, the little pony was nothing in weight compared to the steers, and even if she were, he stood a chance of having his legs crushed. The only hope was to keep the two herds apart. He wheeled Kit. But as the little mare turned and faced the tossing heads and threatening horns, she knew, as did Wilbur instantaneously, that with the force behind them, no single man could stop the impetus of the herd, although only traveling slowly. Indeed, if he tried, he could see that the rear by pressure onwards would force the outside ranks midway down the herd over the edge of the cliff. Kit spun round again almost on one hoof, all but unseating Wilbur.

But even in that brief moment there had been a change, and the boy felt it. The steers were nervous, and, worst of all, he knew that Kit could realize that he himself was frightened. When a horse feels that the rider is frightened, anything is apt to happen. Wilbur's judgment was not gone, but he was ready to yell. The herd behind grew closer and closer. Presently the walk broke into a short trot, the horns of the following bunch of steers appeared at Kit's flanks, a rumbling as of half-uttered bellows was heard from the rear of the herd, and, on the instant, the steers began to run.

CHAPTER XII
ALMOST TRAMPLED TO DEATH

The minute the stampede began Wilbur's nerves steadied, and with voice more than with hand he quieted Kit. It took a moment or two for the front group to break into the running gallop of the frightened steer, and two head of cattle not twenty feet from Wilbur were forced over the edge before the leaders started to run. In this moment the rear bunch closed up solidly and Wilbur was hemmed in.

The pace became terrific, and as they hurtled along the face of the cliff with the precipice below, Wilbur noted to his horror that he was gradually being forced to the outer edge. Being lighter than the steers, the heavier animals were surging ahead alongside the cliff wall, and the little pony with the boy on his back was inch by inch being forced to the verge, of which there was a clear fall now of about one hundred feet. Vainly he looked for a tree overhanging the road into which he could leap; there were no trees. And every few strides he found himself appreciably nearer the edge. Looking back, as far as he could see the steers were crowding, and looking forward the road curved, hiding what might lie before.

His feet were out of the stirrups and well forward, so that, although he had received three or four bruising encounters as the cattle lurched and surged against him, he was unhurt. Several times Kit was hurled from her stride, but she always picked up her feet neatly again. Wilbur could not but admire the little mare, although he felt that there was no hope for them.

Then suddenly, with an angry bellow, a big black steer which had been pushing up on the inside turned his head and tried to gore the pony. There was not room, however, but the action so angered Wilbur that, pulling his six-shooter, he sent a bullet crashing to his brain. The steer gave a wild lurch, but did not fall immediately, and in an instant was forced to the edge and fell into the valley below. Instantly, Kit, even before Wilbur could speak or lay hand on the rein, gave a sidewise jump into the hole made by the place the black steer had occupied. In one stride as much gain away from the dangerous edge had been made as had been lost in the previous half mile.

More at his ease, but for the fearful speed and the danger that Kit might lose her footing, Wilbur looked ahead, talking to the steers around, endeavoring to quiet them, noting that the road was turning more sharply in the valley, although the downward grade was steeper and it was increasingly hard for the little pony to hold up. But as they turned the curve, there, immediately before them, standing in the middle of the road, with their fishing poles over their shoulders, were a man and a boy, evidently entirely ignorant of the danger so rapidly approaching. The bank above was too steep to climb, and the one below straight ninety feet sheer to the creek. To Wilbur it looked like sure death, and a most awful one at that, but he at least was utterly unable to do anything to prevent it, and he shuddered to think that he himself might be trampling with his pony's hoofs on what might be below.

But just as he had in that instant decided that there was no help for it, he suddenly saw Merritt on old Baldy shoot forward like an arrow from a bow stretched to the uttermost. The herd of steers was traveling at a rapid clip, but under the startling influence of combined quirt and spur, and with no room in which to display his bucking propensities, Baldy just put himself to running, and only hit the high spots here and there.

It seemed incredible to Wilbur that any horse could stop, especially on a down grade, at the speed that Baldy was traveling, but just before he reached the man and boy, having previously shouted to warn them, Merritt pulled up with a jerk that brought Baldy clear back on his haunches. Like a flash of light he leaped from the horse and half lifted, half pushed the man into the saddle, tossed the boy up behind him, and then, grabbing hold of the slicker which was tied behind the cantle, he hit old Baldy a slap with the quirt, and down the road they went, not twenty yards ahead of the steers, Baldy carrying on his back the man and the boy, and Merritt, hanging on like grim death, trying to run, taking strides that looked as though he wore seven-leagued boots. The speed was terrific and presently Wilbur noticed that Merritt was keeping both feet together, putting his weight on the saddle, and vaulting along in immense leaps. One moment he was there, but the next moment that Wilbur looked ahead

Baldy was still racing down the road with his double load, but Merritt was nowhere to be seen. It was with a sickening feeling that Wilbur realized that he must have lost his hold, and was in the same peril from which he had saved the man and the boy.

For a few fearful minutes Wilbur watched the ground beneath his horse's feet, but saw no object in the occasional glimpses he could secure of the dusty road. Once again Wilbur found himself being forced to the outer edge of the road, but the cliff was shallowing rapidly, and now they were not more than twenty feet above the valley with the road curving into it in the distance. A couple of hundred feet further on, however, a hillock rose abruptly, coming within four feet of the level of the road, and Wilbur decided to put the pony at it, seeing there was a chance of safety, and that even if they both got bad falls, there was no fear of being trampled.

Allowing the pony to come to the outside, he reined her in hard and led her to the jump, swinging from the saddle as he did so in order to give both Kit and himself a fair chance. The pony, released from the weight of the rider before she struck ground, met it in a fair stride, and without losing footing kept up the gait to the bottom of the hillock, pulling up herself on the level grass below. But Wilbur, not being able to estimate his jump, because he was in the act of vaulting from the saddle, struck the ground all in a heap, crumpled up as though he were broken in pieces and was hurled down the hill, reaching the bottom stunned. He was unconscious for several minutes, but when he came to himself, Kit was standing over him, nosing him with her soft muzzle as though to bring him round. Weakly he staggered to his feet, and seeing Kit standing patiently, managed to clamber into the saddle.

The pony started immediately at an easy canter, crossing the valley and meeting the herd where the road ran into the level. The cattle were tired from the run, and sick and bruised as he was, Wilbur headed them off and rounded them up, being aided presently by Rodgers and Grier, who had found themselves unable to cut into the stampeding herd, and consequently had waited until the whole herd got by, when they had ridden back along the trail a little distance, got down to the creek by a bridle path, and crossed the valley by a short cut.

In the distance Baldy could be seen grazing, and Wilbur lightly touched Kit with the spur to find out what had happened. The bay, as soon as he had stopped running, evidently had bucked off his two riders, who were still sitting on the ground, apparently dazed. The man, who was evidently an Eastern tourist, was pale as ashes and dumb with fright, and could tell nothing. The boy knew no more than, "He had to let go, he had to let go."

Together with Grier, Wilbur started back along the road to look for what might be left of Merritt. The foreman tried to persuade the lad to stay, for he was bleeding from a scalp wound and his left wrist was sorely twisted, if not actually sprained, but Wilbur replied that he had said he was going back to look for Merritt, and go back he would if both arms and legs were broken. Kit, although very much blown, was willing to be taken up the road at a fair gallop, when, just as they turned a corner, they almost ran down the Supervisor, who was walking down the road as unconcernedly as though nothing had happened.

"Oh, Mr. Merritt," cried the boy, "I thought you were dead."

"Cheerful greeting, that," answered the Forester. "No, I'm not dead. You look nearer it than I do."

"But didn't you get run down?"

"Do I look as if I'd been a sidewalk for a thousand steers?" was the disgusted reply. "Don't ask silly questions, Loyle."

But the foreman broke in:

"The boy's right enough to ask," he said; "an' there's no reason why you shouldn't tell. How did you dodge the steers?"

"That was easy enough," said Merritt. "I held on to Baldy until I saw a crack in the rock big enough to hold a man. Then I let go and crawled into that until the herd passed by."

The boy breathed a sigh of relief.

"I sure thought you were gone," he said.

The Supervisor scanned him keenly, then slapped Kit heartily on the flank.

"You've got a good little mare there," he said; "there's not many of them could have done it. Tell me all about it some time. What started them?" he added, turning to the cattleman.

"That fool new bridge gave way just as the last of the bunch crowded on it. About twenty of them fell over the cliff there, and about thirty more along the road. But it might have been a heap worse, an' you ought ter have two life-savin' medals."

Merritt's only reply was a gesture of protest.

"An' you, youngster," went on the cattleman, "you kept your nerve and rode a bully ride. I wish you'd take my quirt and keep it from me as a remembrance of your first experience with a cattle stampede."

Wilbur stammered some words of thanks, but the foreman waved them aside.

"And now," said the Supervisor, with an entire change of tone, "I guess we'll go back and get the pack-horse and go on to the valley."

As they rode over the bridge Wilbur noted with a great deal of interest the breakage of the supporting timbers on the outer side, and looking down into the valley beneath, he could see the bodies of the cattle who had been pushed over the edge in the stampede.

"I read a story once," said the boy, "of a youngster who got caught in a stampede of buffalo, and when his horse lost his footing he escaped by jumping from the back of one buffalo to another until he reached the outside of the herd. But I never believed it much."

"It makes a good yarn," said the Supervisor, "an' it's a little like the story they tell of Buffalo Bill, who, trying to get away from a buffalo stampede, was thrown by his horse puttin' his foot in a badger hole and breaking his leg."

"Why, what in the world did he do?" queried Wilbur.

"He waited until the foremost buffalo was just upon him, then gave a leap, clear over his horns, and landed on his back, then turning sharply round so as to face the head instead of the tail, he pulled out his revolver and kept shooting to one side of the buffalo's head, just past his eye, so that at every shot the beast turned a little more to one side, thus cutting him out of the herd. Then, when he was clear of the herd, he shot the buffalo."

"What for?" asked Wilbur indignantly. "It seems a shame to kill the buffalo which had got him free."

"What chance would he have had against an angered buffalo alone and on foot?" said Merritt. "He couldn't very well get off and make a bow to the beast and have the buffalo drop a curtsey?"

"I hadn't thought of that," said the boy, laughing.

"I was afraid I might have to try that dodge, but when I saw the crack in the rock I knew it was all right."

"Well," said Wilbur as they turned off the road to where the pack-horse had been picketed, "I think we're both pretty lucky to have come off so easily."

Merritt looked at the lad. He was dusty and grimy to a degree, his clothes were torn in a dozen places where he had gone rolling down the hill, a handkerchief was roughly knotted around his head, and there were streaks of dried blood in his hair.

"You look a little the worse for wear," he said; "maybe you'd better go home, and I'll go on alone."

"I won't," said Wilbur.

"You what?" came the curt rebuke. "You mean that you would rather not."

"Yes, sir," said the boy. "I mean that I don't feel too used up."

The Supervisor nodded and rode on ahead. For a couple of miles or so, they rode single file, and in spite of the boy's bold announcement that he was not too badly shaken up, by the time he had ridden nearly an hour more in the hot sun his head was aching furiously and he was beginning to stiffen up. Accordingly he was glad when a cabin hove in sight, and he cantered up to ask if they might call for a drink of water.

"We stop here," was the laconic reply.

As they rode up a big man came out of the house, which was quite a fair-sized place, to meet them.

"Well, Merritt," he said, "what have you got for me this time?" motioning to the boy.

"No patient for you, Doc," said Merritt; "one for your wife."

The mountain doctor laughed, a great big hearty laugh.

"Violet," he called, "you're taking my practice away from me. Here's a patient that says he won't have me, but wants you."

Immediately at his call, a small, slender woman came to the porch of the house, and seeing the doctor helping Wilbur down from the saddle, stepped forward.

"I can walk all right," said Wilbur when the doctor put out a hand to steady him. "I just wanted a drink of water."

"Right you are," said the doctor, "we'll give you all the water you want, just in a minute. Now," he continued as he led the boy into the house, "let's have a look at the trouble."

But Wilbur interposed.

"This Forest Service," he said, smiling, "is the worst that ever happened for having to obey orders, and Mr. Merritt put me in charge of your wife, not you."

The big doctor put his hand on the shoulder of his wife and roared until the house shook with his laughter. It was impossible to resist the infection, and Wilbur, despite his headache, found himself laughing with the rest. But the doctor's wife, stepping quietly forward, took the lad aside and, removing the handkerchief that Grier had wound around his head, bathed the wound and cleansed it. She had just finished this when the doctor came over, still laughing. He touched the wound deftly, and Wilbur was amazed to find that the touch of this large, hearty man was just as soft and tender as that of his wife. There was power in his very finger-tips, and the boy felt it. He looked up, smiling.

"I guess you're Doctor Davis," he said.

"Why?" said the doctor; "what makes you think so?"

"Oh, I just felt it," the boy replied. "I've heard a lot about you."

"I'm 'it,' all right," said the doctor, "but you've refused to allow me to attend you. I'll turn the case over to Dr. Violet Davis," and he laughed again.

Mrs. Davis smiled brightly in response and continued attending to the boy. Then she turned to the two men.

"You've put this case in my charge," she said, "and I'm going to prescribe rest for a day or two anyway. That is," she added, "unless Mr. Merritt finds it compulsory to take him away."

The Supervisor smiled one of his rare smiles.

"I wouldn't be so unkind as to take any one away from here unnecessarily," he said, "no matter how busy. But there always is a lot to do. Ever since the beavers first started forestry, it has meant work, and lots of it. But if you're told to rest you've got to do it. I know. I've been sick myself here."

The doctor slapped him on the shoulder.

"Beautiful case," he said, "beautiful case. But he wouldn't obey orders."

"He always did mine," put in Mrs. Davis.

"I'm afraid I can't this time," said the Supervisor with one of his abrupt changes of manner, turning to the door. "I'll call for Loyle on my way home to-morrow."

"Oh, Mr. Merritt," began Mrs. Davis in protest, "he ought to have two or three days' rest, anyway."

The chief of the forest turned to Wilbur.

"Well?" he queried.

The boy looked around at the comfortable home, at the big jovial doctor, and his charming little wife, and thought how delightful it would be to have a few days' rest. And his head was aching, and he was very stiff. Then he looked at the Supervisor, quiet and unflinching in anything that was to be done, working with him and helping him despite the big interests for which he was responsible, he thought of the Forest Service to which he was pledged to serve, he remembered his little tent home and the portion of the range over which he had control, and straightened up.

"What time to-morrow?" he said. "I'll be ready."

"Middle of the afternoon," said Merritt. "So long."

He bade good-by to the doctor and his wife, and after having seen that Kit was properly attended to, went on his way to the Kern River Valley, to visit the Edison power plant erected on the river, and to prepare for the installation of the new pulp-mill.

In the meantime, Wilbur, more fatigued by the day's excitement than he had supposed himself to be, had fallen asleep, a sleep unbroken until the evening. And all evening the doctor and his wife told him stories of the Forest Service men and of the various miners, lumbermen, prospectors, ranchers, and so forth, all tales of manliness, courage, and endurance, and not infrequently of heroism. But when Wilbur told of the professor and asked about other greenhorns that had come to the forest, the doctor turned and asked him if he knew anything of "the boy from Peanutville."

"He had just come into camp up here in the Sierras," said the doctor on receiving the lad's negative reply, "from some little place in the middle West that was giving itself airs as a city. He had read somewhere about the forest Rangers, and he himself had been on several Sunday School picnics in the woods, so he thought that he knew all about it. At the end of his first couple of days' work he said:

"'I never supposed that a Ranger had to cut brush and build fence and grub stumps and slave like a nigger. I don't believe he ought to. I don't think it's what my people would like to have me do. I always supposed that he just rode around under the trees and made outsiders toe the mark.'

"I said he was a new Guard," the doctor continued, "but he said this in camp to a group of old-timers with whom he had been working. They hadn't worried him at all, but had given him a fair show and helped him all they could. But this was too rich. They glanced at each other with mingled contempt and amusement, then put on mournful faces, looked on him solemn-eyed, and regretted the cruelties of the Service.

"'The boss,' they said, 'just sticks it on us all the time. We are workin' like slaves—Guards and Rangers and everybody. It's plumb wicked the way we're herded here.'

"So the new hand felt comforted by this outward sympathy, and he ambled innocently on.

"'That heavy brush tears my clothes, and my back aches, and I burned a shoe, and my socks are full of stickers. Then I fell on the barbed wire when I was stretching it—and cut my nose. I tell you what it is, fellows, if I ever get a chance to get away, I hope I'll never see another inch of barbed wire as long as I live. If I was only back in Peanutville, where I used to live, I could be eating a plate of ice cream this minute instead of working like a dog and having to wash my own clothes Sundays when I might be hearing the band play in the park.'

"'Too bad,' shouted the old Rangers in chorus, until a peal of laughter that echoed through and through that mountain camp showed the indignant youngster that his point of view hadn't been what you might say warmly welcomed by the old-timers.

"But the following day, as I heard the story from Charles H. Shinn," the doctor went on, "one of the best men in the gang took the lad aside the following morning as they were riding up the trail, and said to him:

"'How much of that stuff you was preachin' last night did you mean? Of course, this is hard work; it has to be. Either leave it mighty pronto, or wrastle with it till you're a man at the game. I've seen lots of young fellows harden up—some of 'em just as green an' useless when they came as you are now. Don't you know you hold us back, and waste our time, too, on almost any job? But it's the price we have to pay up here to get new men started. Unless you grow to love it so much that there isn't anything else in all the world you'd care to do, you ain't fit for it, an' you'd better get out, and let some one with more sand than you have get in.'

"Well, Loyle," the doctor said, "that youngster was provoked. He wasn't man enough to get really angry, so that his temper would keep him sticking to the work; he was one of these saucy slap-'em-on-the-wrist-naughty kind.

"'I think all of you are crazy,' he said.

"He walked into the Supervisor's office that afternoon and explained that the kind of work he had been given to do was altogether below his intellectual powers. He never understood how quickly things happened, but he signed a resignation blank almost before he knew it, and went back to Peanutville.

"It so happened that one of the Rangers had friends in Peanutville, and the boys at the camp followed the youth's career with much interest. He clerked, he took money at a circus window, he tried cub newspaper work, he stood behind a dry-goods counter, he was everything by turns but nothing long."

"What finally happened to him?" asked Wilbur.

"Last I heard he was a salesman in a woman's shoe store. But he's still with us in spirit," said the doctor, "as a horrible example. Right now, down in the heart of a forest fire, when the Rangers are working like men possessed down some hot gulch, one will say to the other:

"'Gee, Jack, if I was only back where I used to be, I could be having a plate of ice cream this minute.' And the other will reply: 'I wish I might be back in Peanutville and hear the band play in the park.' And both men will laugh and go at the work all the harder for realizing what a miserable failure the weak greenhorn had been."

"I'm thinking," said Wilbur, "that I'll never give them the chance to talk like that about me!"

"From what I heard," said the doctor, "I don't believe you will."

"And from what I see," said the doctor's wife gently, as the two rose and bade the "patient" good-night, "I know we shall all be glad that you have come to us here in the forest."

CHAPTER XIII

HOW THE FOREST WON A GREAT DOCTOR

In the middle of the night the telephone bell rang. Instantly Wilbur heard the doctor's voice responding.

"Yes, where is it?" he queried. "Where? Oh, just beyond Basco Aleck's place. All right, I'll start right away."

There was some rummaging in the other rooms, and in less than five minutes' time the clatter of hoofs outside told the boy that the doctor was off, probably on the huge gray horse Wilbur had seen in the corral as he rode in that day. It was broad daylight when he wakened again, and Mrs. Davis was standing beside him with his breakfast tray. It was so long since Wilbur had not had to prepare breakfast for himself that he felt quite strange, but the night's rest had eased him wonderfully, and aside from a little soreness where he had had his scalp laid open, he was quite himself again.

"Did Doctor Davis have to go away in the night?" he asked. "I thought I heard the telephone."

"Yes," answered the doctor's wife. "But that is nothing new. Almost once a week, at least, he is sent for in the night, or does not reach home till late in the night. I've grown used to it," she added; "doctors' wives must."

"But distances are so great, and there are so few trails," said the boy, "and Doctor Davis is so famous, one would think that he would do better in a city."

"Better for himself?" came the softly uttered query.

The boy colored hotly as he realized the idea of selfishness that there had been in his speech.

"I beg your pardon," he said. "No, I see. But it does seem strange, just the same, that he should be out here."

"He wouldn't be happy anywhere else."

"Excuse me, Mrs. Davis," said the boy, who had caught something of the Supervisor's abruptness, "but what brought him here?"

"Do you not," answered the doctor's wife, giving question for question, "know the old hunter, 'Rifle-Eye Bill'? I don't know his right name. Why, of course, you must; he's the Ranger in your part of the forest."

"Do I know him?" said Wilbur, and without stopping for further question talked for ten minutes on end, telling all that the old hunter had done for him and how greatly he admired him. "Know him," he concluded, "I should just guess I did."

"It was he," said the woman, "who persuaded us to come out here."

"Won't you tell me?" pleaded the boy. "I'd love to hear anything about Rifle-Eye. And the doctor, too," he added as an afterthought.

"It was long ago," she began, "seventeen years ago. Yes," she continued with a smile at the lad's surprise, "I have lived here seventeen years."

"Do you —" began the boy excitedly, "do you ride a white mare?"

This time it was the doctor's wife who colored. She flushed to the roots of her hair.

"Yes," she answered hurriedly, and went on to explain the early conditions of the forest. But Wilbur was not listening, he was remembering the stories that he had heard since his arrival into the forest of the "little white lady," of whom the ranchers and miners always spoke so reverently. But presently Rifle-Eye's name attracted his attention and he listened again.

"We were camping," she said, "in one of the redwood groves not far from San Francisco for the summer, the doctor having been appointed an attending surgeon at one of the larger hospitals, although he was very young. We had been married only a little over a year. One evening just after supper, Rifle-Eye, although we did not know him then, walked into camp.

"'You are a doctor, an operating doctor?' he inquired.

"'Yes,' my husband replied, 'I am a surgeon.'

"Then the old hunter came to where I was standing.

"'You are a doctor's wife?' he queried. You know that direct way of his?"

"Indeed I do," Wilbur replied. "It's one you've got to answer."

"So I said, 'Yes, I am a doctor's wife,' just as if I was a little girl answering a catechism.

"'The case is seventy miles away,' he said, 'and there's a horse saddled.' He turned to me. 'A woman I know is coming over in a little while to stay the night with you, so that you will not be lonely. Come, doctor.' There was a hurried farewell, and they were gone. I can laugh now, as I think of it, but it was dreadful then.

"Presently, however, the woman that he had spoken of came over to our camp. She was a mountaineer's wife, and very willing and helpful. But I was a little frightened, as I had never seen any one quite like her before."

"You couldn't have had much in common," said Wilbur, who was observant enough to note the artistic nature of the room wherein he lay, the exquisite cleanliness and freshness of all his surroundings, and the faultless English of the doctor's wife. Besides, she was pretty and sweet-looking, and boys are quick to note it.

"We didn't," she answered, "but when I happened to mention the old hunter, why the woman was transformed. She brightened up, and told me tales far into the night of what the old hunter had done until," she smiled, "I almost thought he must be as nice as Doctor Davis."

"Doctor Davis does look awfully fine," agreed Wilbur.

"I always think so," said his wife demurely. "Two days passed before the men returned, and when I got a chance alone with my husband, he was twice as bad as the mountaineer's wife. He would talk of nothing but Rifle-Eye and the need of surgical work in the mountains.

"'And you, Violet,' he said, 'you're going to ride there with me to-day and help look after this man.' It did rather surprise me, because I knew that he hated to have me troubled with any details of his work, for he used to like to leave his profession behind when he came home. So I knew that he thought it important, and I went. But I rode the greater part of the day with the old hunter, and long before he reached the place where the man was who needed me, all my objections had vanished and I was eager to begin."

"That's just the way that Rifle-Eye does," said the boy, "he makes it seem that what he wants you to do is just what you want to do yourself."

"When I got to the place," she went on, "I found that it was a Basque shepherd, who had been hurt by some of the cattlemen. That made it much more interesting for me, for you know, my people were Basques, that strange old race, who, tradition tells, are all that are left of the shepherds on the mountains of the lost Atlantis. So I nursed him as best I could, and presently, from far and wide over the Rockies I would get messages from the Basque shepherds."

"Didn't you put a stop to the feuds at one time?" asked Wilbur. "The old hunter told me something about 'the little white lady' and the sheep war."

"I helped in many of them," she said simply, "and when they came to me for advice I tried to give it. Doctor Davis was always there to suggest the more advisable course, and I put it to these Bascos, as they called them, so that they would understand."

"How about Burleigh?" asked Wilbur.

But the doctor's wife disclaimed all knowledge of a sheep-owner called Burleigh.

"All right," said Wilbur, "then I'll give my share of the story, as the old hunter told it to me. That is, if you don't mind."

"Tell it," she smiled, "if you like."

"Well," said Wilbur, "one Sunday afternoon a Ranger, whose cabin was near a lookout point, said to his wife, 'I'll ride up to the peak, and be back in time for supper.' He went off in his shirt-sleeves, bare-headed, for an hour's ride, and was gone a week. Up in the brush he found the trail of a band of sheep, and although he was cold and hungry and his horse was playing out, he stuck right on the job until it got too dark to see. The second day he smashed in the door of a miner's cabin, got some grub, and nailed a note on the door saying who'd taken it, and kept on. He tired his horse out, and left him in another fellow's corral, but kept on going on foot. The sheepman was known as dangerous, but this little Ranger—did I tell you he was Irish—stuck to it, trusting to find some way out even if the grazer did get ugly.

"At last he came on the sheep in a mountain meadow, and Burleigh on his horse by them, a rifle across his saddle bow. The Ranger said little at the time, and the two men went home to supper. After eating, as they sat there, the Ranger said his say. He told the grazer what were the orders he had, and that he would have to live up to them. But the grazer had a copy of 'orders,' too, and he had hired a lawyer to find out how he could get out of them. So he lit into the Ranger.

"'You see, Mac,' he said, 'those orders don't mean anything. They may be all right in Washington, but they don't go here. You can't stop me, nor arrest me, nor hurt my sheep. Your bosses won't stand by you if you get into any mix-up. The best thing you can do is to stay here to-night, and then go home. Make a report on it, if you like, I don't care.'"

"And then the Ranger began," the boy went on. "The old hunter told me that this little bit of an Irishman told the grazer about his work as a Ranger. He told him how he had seen the good that was going to be done, and that having put his hand to the plow, he couldn't let it go again. He didn't know much about it, and he'd never tried to talk about it before, but the natural knack of talking which his race always has came to help him out. Then he began to talk of the sheep and cattle war, and the shame that it was to have them killing each other's flocks and shooting each other because they could not agree about the right to grass.

"'An' there's one more thing,' he said, "tis only the other day that I was talkin' to the "little white lady," and she said she knew that you wouldn't be the one to start up trouble again.' And he wound up with an appeal to his better judgment, which, so the old hunter told me the grazer said afterward, would have got a paralyzed mule on the move.

"When he got through, Burleigh merely answered:

"'Mac, take that blanket and go to bed. I'll talk to you in the morning.'

"When the Ranger woke, a little after daylight, the grazer sat beside his blanket, smoking. He began without wasting any time.

"'Mac,' he said, 'I'm going to take my sheep out to-day. Not because of any of your little bits of printed orders—I could drive a whole herd through them; and not because of any of your bosses back in Washington, who wouldn't know a man's country if they ever got into it, and couldn't find their way out; and not entirely because, as you say, "the little white lady" trusts me, though perhaps that's got a good deal to do with it. But when I find a man who is so many different kinds of a fool as you seem to be, it looks some like my moral duty to keep him out of an asylum.' And that's the story I heard about Burleigh.

"But I interrupted you," the boy continued, "you were going to tell me about Doctor Davis. Didn't you ever go back to the city?"

"Oh, yes," she replied. "The doctor had to take his hospital service, and for three years he spent six months in the hospital in the city, and six months out here in the mountains. But there were several good surgeons in the city, and only one on the great wide Sierras, and, as you know, he is strong enough for the hardest work. So,—I remember well the night,—he came to me, and hesitatingly suggested that we should live out here for always, but that he didn't wish to take me away from my city friends. And I—oh, I had been wanting to come all the time. I was just one out of so many in the city, paying little social calls, but here I found so many people to be fond of. I think I know every one on the mountains here, and they are all so kind to me. And," she added proudly, "so appreciative of the doctor."

Wilbur laughed as she gathered up the things on the tray.

"Well," he said, "I don't believe the old hunter ever did a better thing when he got Doctor Davis to come to the forest—unless, it was the day 'the little white lady' came with him. Haven't I had a broken head, and am I not her patient? You bet!"

But Mrs. Davis only smiled as she passed from the room.

Wilbur spent the rest of the morning in the doctor's library, and was more than delighted to learn that these books were there for borrowing, on the sole condition that they should be returned. He learned, later, that under the guise of a library to lend books, all sorts of little plans were done for the cheering of the lives of those who lived in isolated portions of the mountain range. The boy had not been twenty-four hours under the doctor's roof, yet he was quite at home, and sorry to go when the Supervisor rode up. He had been careful to groom Kit very thoroughly, and she was standing saddled at the door, half an hour before the time appointed. He was ready to swing into the saddle as soon as Merritt appeared.

"Not so fast, Loyle," he said, "this is once that promptness is a bad thing. I must have a word or two with Mrs. Davis; he'd be a pretty poor stick who ever missed that chance."

So, while he went inside, Wilbur looked over the pack to see that it was riding easily, and led Baldy to where he could have a few mouthfuls of grass. And when he came out the Forester was even more silent than usual, and rode for two hours without uttering a syllable.

"Did you find everything going on all right for the pulp-mill?" asked Wilbur, finally desiring to give a chance for conversation. But Merritt simply replied, "Fairly so," and relapsed into silence. He wakened into sudden energy, however, when, a half an hour later, in making a shortcut to headquarters he came upon an old abandoned trail. It was somewhat overgrown, but the Supervisor turned into it and followed it for some length, finally arriving at a large spring, one of the best in the forest, which evidently had been known at some time prior to the Forest Service taking control, but now had passed into disuse. But Merritt was even more surprised to find beside the spring a prospector of the old type, with his burro and pack, evidently making camp for the night.

"Evenin'," said Merritt, "where did you get hold of this trail?"

"Allers knew about it," said the prospector. "I s'pose," he added, noting the bronze "U. S." on the khaki shirt, "that you're the Ranger."

"Supervisor," replied Merritt. "Locating a mineral claim, are you?"

"Not yet," the other replied; "I ain't located any mineral to claim yet. I'll come to you for a permit as soon as I do. But I'm lookin' for Burns's lost mine."

"You don't believe in that old yarn, surely?" questioned the other surprisedly.

"Would I be lookin' for it if I hadn't doped it out that it was there?"

"Where?"

"Oh, somewheres around here. I reckon it's further north. But if you don't take any stock in it, there's no use talkin'."

"I'm not denying its existence," said Merritt, "but you know dozens of men have looked for that and no one's found it yet."

"There can't be but one find it," said the prospector. "I aims to be that one. I used to think it was further south. Twenty years ago I spent a lot o' time down at the end of the range. Two seasons ago I got a hunch it was further north. I couldn't get away last year, so here I am. I've been busy on Indian Creek for some years."

"Got a claim there?"

"Got the only jade in the country."

"Was it you located that mine in the Klamath Forest?" queried the Supervisor interestedly. "But that's quite a good deposit. I shouldn't think you'd be prospecting now."

"I didn't for two years. But, pard, it was dead slow, an' so I hired a man to run the works while I hit the old trail again. I don't have to get anybody to grubstake me now. I've been able to boost some of the others who used to help me."

"But what started you looking for Burns's mine? I thought that story had been considered a fake years ago."

"What is a lost mine?" asked Wilbur.

Merritt looked at him a moment thoughtfully, then turned to the prospector.

"You tell the yarn," he said. "You probably know it better than I do."

"I'm not much on talkin'," began the prospector. "Away back in the sixties, after the first gold-rush, Jock Burns, one of the old Forty-niners, started prospectin' in the Sierras. There's not much here, but one or two spots pay. By an' by Burns comes into the settlements with a few little bags of gold dust, an' nuggets of husky size. He blows it all in. He spends free, but he's nowise wasteful, so he stays in town maybe a month.

"Then he disappears from view, an' turns up in less than another month in town with another little bundle of gold dust. It don't take much figurin' to see that where there's a pay streak so easy worked as that, there's a lot more of it close handy. An' so they watches Burns close. Burns, he can't divorce himself from his friends any more than an Indian can from his color. This frequent an' endurin' friendliness preys some on Burns's nature, an' bein' of a bashful disposition, he makes several breaks to get away. But while the boys are dead willin' to see him start for the mountains, they reckon an escort would be an amiable form of appreciation. Also, they ain't got no objection to bein' shown the way to the mine.

"Burns gets a little thin an' petered out under the strain, but time an' agin he succeeds in givin' 'em the slip. Sure enough he lines up a month or two later with some more of the real thing. Finally, one of these here friends gets a little peevish over his frequent failures to stack the deck on Burns. He avers that he'll insure that Burns don't spend any more coin until he divvys up, an' accordin'ly he hands him a couple of bullets where he thinks they'll do most good."

"What did he want to kill him for?" asked Wilbur.

"He didn't aim to kill him prompt," was the reply. "His idee was to trot him down the hill by easy stages, an' gradooally indooce the old skinflint to talk. But his shootin' was a trifle too straight, and Burns jest turns in his toes then an' there. This displeases the sentiment of the community. Then some literary shark gits up and spins a yarn about killin' some goose what laid eggs that assayed a hundred per cent., an' they decides that it would be a humane thing to arrange that Burns shan't go out into the dark without some comfortin' friend beside him. So they dispatches the homicide, neat an' pretty, with the aid of a rope, an' remarks after the doin's is over that Burns is probably a heap less lonesome."

"Well, I should think that would have stopped all chance of further search," said Wilbur.

"It did. But a year or two after that, Burns acquires the habit of intrudin' his memory on the minds of some of these here friends. When it gits noised about that a certain kind of nose-paint is some advantageous toward this particular brand of dream, why, there ain't no way of keeping a sufficient supply in camp. I goes up against her myself, an' wild licker she is. But one by one, the boys all gets to dreamin' that Burns has sorter floated afore them, accordin' to ghostly etiquette, an' pointed a ghostly finger at the ground. Which ain't so plumb exact, for no one supposes a mine to be up in the air. But different ones affirms that they can recognize the features of the landscape which the ghost of Burns frequents. As, however, they all strikes out in different directions, I ain't takin' no stock therein.

"But, two years ago, when I was meanderin' around lookin' for signs, I comes across the bones of an old mule with the remains of a saddle on his back, an' I didn't have any trouble in guessin' it to be Burns's. There was no way of tellin', though, whether he was goin' or returnin' when the mule broke down, or if he was far or near the mine, but, anyhow, it gave some idee of direction, an' I reckon I'm goin' to find it."

"All right," said the Supervisor as they shook up their horses ready to go, "I hope you have good luck and find it."

"I'll let you or Rifle-Eye know as soon as I do," called back the prospector, "an' you folks can pan out some samples. If I find it, we'll make the Yukon look sick."

Merritt laughed as they cantered down the trail to headquarters.

CHAPTER XIV
A ROLLING CLOUD OF SMOKE

The days became hotter and hotter, and each morning when Wilbur rose he searched eagerly for some sign of cloud that should presage rain, but the sky remained cloudless. Several times he had heard of fires in the vicinity, but they had kept away from that portion of the forest over which he had control, and he had not been summoned from his post. The boy had given up his former schedule of covering his whole forest twice a week, and now was riding on Sundays, thus reaching every lookout point every other day. It was telling upon the horses, and he himself was conscious of the strain, but he was more content in feeling that he had gone the limit in doing the thing that was given him to do.

One day, while in a distant part of the forest, he came upon the signs of a party of campers. Since his experience with the tourists the boy had become panic-stricken by the very idea of careless visitors to the forest, and the chance of their setting a fire, and so, recklessly, he put his horse at a sharp gallop and started down the trail that they had left. The signs were new, so that he overtook them in a couple of hours. But in the meantime he had passed the place where the party had made their noonday halt, and he could see that full precautions had been taken to insure the quenching of the fire.

When he overtook them, moreover, he was wonderfully relieved and freed from his fears. There were six in all, the father, who was quite an old man, the mother, two grown-up sons, and two younger girls. They had heard his horse come galloping down the trail, and the two younger men had hung back to be the first to meet him.

"Which way?" one of them asked, as Wilbur pulled his horse down to a walk.

"Your way," said Wilbur, "I guess. I just rode down to see who it was on the trail. There was a bunch of tourists hanging around here a few weeks ago, and the forest floor is too dry to take any chances with their campfires."

"Oh, that's it," said the former speaker. Then, with a laugh, he continued: "I guess we aren't in that class."

"I can see you're not," the boy replied, "but I'm one of the Forest Service men, and it's a whole lot better to be safe than sorry."

"Right," the other replied. "I think you might ride on with us a bit," he continued, "and talk to the rest of them. It may ease their minds. You were headed our way down that trail as though you were riding for our scalps."

Wilbur laughed at the idea of his inspiring fear in the two stalwart men riding beside him.

"I guess I'd have had some job," he said, "if I had tried it on."

"Well," the first speaker answered, "we wouldn't be the first of the family to decorate a wigwam that way. My grandfather an' his two brothers got ambushed by some Apaches in the early seventies."

"Your grandfather?" the boy repeated.

"Sure, son. Most of the fellows that got the worst of it with the Indians was some one's granddad, I reckon. One of my uncles, father's brother, was with them at the time, and he got scalped, too. It isn't so long ago since the days of the Indians, son, an' it's wonderful to think of the families livin' peacefully where the war-parties used to ride. That's goin' to be a great country down there. But," he broke off suddenly, "here's dad."

The bent figure in the saddle, riding an immense iron gray mare, straightened up as the three rode close, and the old man turned a keen glance on the boy. Instantly, Wilbur was reminded of the old hunter, although the two men were as unlike as they could be, and in that same instant the boy realized that the likeness lay in the eyes. The springiness might have gone out of his step, and to a certain extent the seat in the saddle was unfirm, and the strength and poise of the body showed signs of abatement, but the fire in the eyes was undimmed and every line of the features was instinct to a wonderful degree with life and vitality. After a question or two to his sons he turned to the boy, and in response to a query as to his destination, replied, in a sing-song voice that was reminiscent of frontier camp-meetings:

"I'm goin' to the Promised Land. It's been a long an' a weary road, but the time of rejoicin' has come. It is writ that the desert shall blossom as a rose, an' I'm goin' to grow rose-trees where the cactus used to be; the solitary place shall be alone no more, an' I and mine are flockin' into it; the lion an' wolf shall be no more therein, an' the varmints all are gone away; an' a little child shall lead them, an' before I die I reckon to see my children an' my children's children under the shadow of my vine an' fig tree."

Wilbur looked a little bewilderedly at the two younger men and one of them said hastily:

"We're goin' down to the Salt River Valley, down in Arizona, where the government has irrigated land."

"Oh, I know," said Wilbur, "that's one of the big projects of the Reclamation Service."

"Have you been down there at all?"

"No," the boy answered, "but I understand that to a very great extent much of the Forest Service work is being done with irrigation in view."

"They used to call it," broke out the old prophet again, "the 'land that God forgot,' but now they're callin' it the 'land that God remembered.'"

Wilbur waited a moment to see if the old man would speak again, but as he was silent, he turned to the man beside him:

"How did you get interested in this land?" he asked.

"I was born," the other answered, "in one of the villages of the cliff-dwellers, who lived so many years ago. Dad, he always used to think that the sudden droppin' out of those old races an' the endurin' silence about them was some kind of a visitation. An' he always believed that the curse, whatever it was, would be taken off."

"That's a queer idea," said the boy; "I never heard it before."

"Well," said the other, "it does seem queer. An' when the government first started this reclamation work, dad he thought it was a sign, and he went into every project, I reckon, the government ever had. An' they used to say

156

that unless 'the Apache Prophet,' as they called him, had been once on a project, it was no use goin' on till he came."

"But what did he do?"

"They always gave him charge of a gang of men for as long as he wanted it, and Jim an' I, we used to boss a gang, too. We've been on the Huntley and Sun River in Montana, we've laid the foundation of the highest masonry dam in the world—the Shoshone dam in Wyoming,—helped build a canal ninety-five miles long in Nebraska, I've driven team on the Belle Fourche in South Dakota; in Kansas, where there's no surface water, I've dug wells that with pumps will irrigate eight thousand acres, and away down in New Mexico on the Pecos and in Colorado on the Rio Grande I've helped begin a new life for those States."

"An' a river shall flow out of it," the old man burst forth again, "an' I reckon thar ain't a river flowin' nowhere that's forgot. I don't know where Jordan rolls, but any stream that brings smilin' plenty where the desert was before looks enough like Jordan to suit me. I've seen it, I tell you," he added fiercely, turning to the boy, "I've seen the desert an' I've seen Eden, an' I'm goin' there to live. An' where the flamin' sword of thirst once whirled, there's little brooks a-ripplin' an' the flowers is springin' fair."

"You must have seen great changes?" suggested the boy, interested in the old man's speech.

"Five years ago," he answered, "we were campin' on the Snake River, in southern Idaho. There was sage-brush, an' sand, an' stars, an' nothin' else. An engineerin' fellow, who he was I dunno, rides up to the fire. Where he comes from I dunno; I reckon his body came along the road of the sage-brush and the sand, but his mind came by the stars. An' he takes the handle of an ax, and draws out on the sand an irrigatin' plan. There wasn't a house for thirty miles. An' he just asks if he shall go ahead. An' I knows he's right, an' I says I knows he's right, an' he goes straight off to Washington, an' now there's three thousand people where the sage-brush was, and right on the very spot where my campfire smoked just five years ago, a school has been opened with over a hundred children there."

He stopped as suddenly as he began.

"There was some great work in the Gunnison canyon, was there not?" queried Wilbur.

The old man made no reply, and the son answered the question.

"When they had to lower a man from the top into the canyon, seven hundred feet below," he said, "Dad was the first to volunteer. I reckon, son, there's no greater story worth the tellin' than the Uncompahgre tunnel. And then, I ain't told nothin' about the big Washington and Oregon valleys, where tens of thousands now have homes an' are rearin' the finest kind of men an' women. But, as dad says, we're comin' home. There's four centuries of our history and there's seven centuries of Moki traditions, an' still there's nothing to tell me who the people are who built the cliff-town where I was born. Dad, he thinks that when the water comes, perhaps the stones will speak. I don't know, but if they ever do, I want to be there to hear. It's the strangest, wildest place in all the world, I think, and while it is harsh and unkindly, still it's home. Dad's right there. These forests are all right," he added, remembering that the boy was attached to the Forest Service, "but for me, I want a world whose end you can't see an' where every glance leads up."

"Do you suppose," said Wilbur, "that in the days of the cliff-dwellers, and earlier, the 'inland empire' was densely populated?"

"Some time," the other replied slowly, "it must have been. Not far from my cliff home is the famous Cheltro Palace, which contains over thirty million blocks of stone."

"How big is it?" asked Wilbur.

"Well, it is four stories high, nearly five hundred feet long, an' just half that width."

Wilbur whistled.

"My stars," he ejaculated, "that is big! And is there nothing left to tell about them?" he asked.

The other shook his head.

"Nothing," he answered.

"They were, an' they were not," interjected the old patriarch. "I looked for the place where I should find him, an' lo, he was gone. They were eatin' an' drinkin' when the end came, an' they knew it not. Like enough they had some warnin' which they heeded not, an' their house is left unto them desolate. An' we go in and possess their land. Young man, come with us."

Wilbur started.

"Oh, I can't," he said. "I should like to see some of those projects, but my work is here. But I'm one of you," he added eagerly; "the rivers that flow down to enrich your desert rise from springs in our mountains, and all those springs would dry up if the forests were destroyed. And all the headwaters of the streams are in our care."

"You kind of look after them when they're young," Wilbur's companion suggested, "that we can use them when the time is ripe."

"That is just it," said Wilbur. Then, turning to the old man, he added:

"I must go back to my patrol," he said, "but when you're down in that Garden of Eden, where the river is making the world all over again, you'll remember us once in a while, and the little bit of a stream that flows out of my corral will always have good wishes for you down there."

The old man turned in his saddle with great dignity.

"There be vessels to honor," he said gravely, "an' to every one his gifts. Go back to your forest home an' work, an' take an old man's wishes that while water runs you may never want for work worth doin', for friends worth havin', an' at the last a tally you ain't ashamed to show."

Wilbur raised his hat in salute for reply and reined Kit in until the party was lost to view. The afternoon was drawing on and the lad had lost nearly two hours in following the party, and in his chat with the old patriarch, but he could not but feel that even the momentary glimpse he had been given of the practical workings of the reclamation work of the government had gone far to emphasize and render of keener personal interest all that he had learned at school or heard from the Forest Service men about the making of a newer world within the New World itself. And when he remembered that over a quarter of a million families, within a space of about six years, have made their homes on what was an absolute desert ten years ago, and that these men and women were stirred with the same spirit as the old patriarch, he felt, as he had said, that the conserving of the mountain streams was work worth while.

As it chanced, he passed over the little stream whose channel he had cleared on one of his patrol rides, and he stopped a moment to look at it.

"Well," he said aloud, "I suppose some youngster some day will be picking oranges off a tree that would have died if I hadn't done that day's work," and he rode on to his camp greatly pleased with himself.

For a day or two the boy found himself quite unable to shake the spell of the old patriarch's presence off his mind, and the more he thought over it, the more he realized that scarcely any one thing in the whole of the United States loomed larger on its future than the main idea of Conservation. It had been merely a word before, but now it was a reality, and he determined to take the first opportunity he would have, during his vacation, of going down to the Salt River Valley to see the old patriarch once again.

And still the weather grew hotter and the sky remained cloudless. And now, every evening, Rifle-Eye would telephone over to make sure that Wilbur was back at camp and that there was as yet no danger. They had had one quite sharp tussle at a distant point of the forest, and one day Wilbur had received orders to make a long ride to a lookout point in another part of the forest, the work of a Guard who had been called away to fight fire, but so far, Wilbur had been free. Two or three times he found himself waking suddenly in the night, possessed with an intense desire to saddle Kit and ride off to a part of the forest where he had either dreamed or thought a fire was burning, but Rifle-Eye had been careful to warn him against this very thing, and although the morning found him simply wild to ride to this point of supposed danger, he had followed orders and ridden his regular round.

Although Wilbur's camp was high, the heat grew hard to bear, and when the boy passed from the shade of the pine along the naked rock to some lookout point the ground seemed to blaze under him. The grass was rapidly turning brown in the exposed places, and the pine needles were as slippery as the smoothest ice.

Just at noon, one morning, Wilbur turned his horse—he was not riding Kit that day—into one of these open trails, and taking out his glasses, commenced to sweep the horizon. A heat haze was abroad, and his over-excited eyes seemed to see smoke everywhere. But, as he swept round the horizon, suddenly his whole figure stiffened. He looked long, then, with a sigh of relief, turned away, and completed his circuit of the horizon. This done, he directed the glasses anew where he had looked before. He looked long, unsatisfied, then lay down on the rock where he could rest the glasses and scanned the scene for several minutes.

"Be sure," Merritt had once warned him, "better spend a half an hour at the start than lose two hours later."

But Wilbur felt sure and rushed for his horse. Half-way he paused. Then, going deliberately into the shade of a heavy spruce, he half-closed his eyes for a minute or two to let the muscles relax. Then quietly he came to the edge of the cliff, and directing his glasses point-blank at the place he had been examining so closely, scanned it in every detail. He slipped the glasses back into their case, snapped the clasp firmly, walked deliberately back to his horse, who had been taking a few mouthfuls of grass, tightened the cinches, looked to it that the saddle was resting true and that the blanket had not rucked up, vaulted into the saddle, and rode to the edge of the cliff. There was no doubt of it. Hanging low in the heavy air over and through the dark foliage of pine and spruce was a dull dark silver gleam, which changed enough as the sunlight fell upon it to show that it was eddying vapor rather than the heavier waves of fog.

"Smoke!" he said. "We've got to ride for it."

CHAPTER XV

THE FOREST ABLAZE

As Wilbur broke into a steady, if fast pace, it seemed to him that all his previous experiences in the forest had been directed to this one end. True, once before, he had seen smoke in the distance and had ridden to it, but then he had felt that it was a small fire which he would be able to put out, as indeed it had proved. But now, while there was no greater cloud of smoke visible than there had been before, the boy felt that this was in some measure different.

As his horse's hoofs clattered on the trail, it seemed to his excited fancy that every inch of ground was crying to the valley below, "He's coming," the wind that blew past him seemed filled with purpose, every eddying gust awoke in him a greater desire to reach the place of danger before the wind should rise to higher gusts, and as the needles of the pines whispered overhead it seemed to Wilbur that they murmured, "Hurry, hurry, if you want to be there on time." Over and over again, he found himself on the point of using the whip or spurs to induce a greater burst of speed, but as often as he did so, the old short, curtly-worded counsels of Merritt came back to him, never to press his horse if the ride was to be of any length, and he grew to believe that the animal knew as well as the rider the errand on which he was bound.

He had thought, before starting, of riding back to his camp and telephoning to Rifle-Eye, but the knowledge that after all it might be a little fire kept him back. All the tales that he had ever heard about forest fires rushed through his mind, but he resolutely set them aside to watch his horse's path, to hold him in where he would be apt to stumble, to give him his head on rising ground, and to bring him to speed where the trail was easy to follow. Two hours he rode, his horse well in hand, until he came to the place where he had decided from his lookout point that he would have to leave the trail and plunge through the forest itself.

This was a very different matter, and Wilbur found himself wondering how his horse kept his footing. He was not riding Kit, for which he was glad, as in leaving the trail and plunging downhill he had struck some parts of the forest where undergrowth was present, and his favorite mare's slender legs would have been badly scratched. Also the footing grew dangerous and uncertain. There had been many windfalls in the forest, and now was no time to take them quietly; a flying leap, not knowing what might be on the other side, a stumble, perhaps, which sent the boy's heart into his mouth, a quick recovery, and they were off again, only to find, perhaps, a few yards further on, a bowlder-strewn gully which it would have been madness to take at other than a walk. But the boy chafed terribly at each and every stay to his ride, and he had to hold himself in hand as much as he had his horse.

Little by little the exhilaration of the ride stole into his veins. He was alone in the forest, he and his horse, the world was all before, and he must ride and ride. He shouted as he rode under the towering pines, raced across a clearing with a whoop that roused the echoes, and yelled for sheer delight in the mad ride through the untraveled forest, where, as the knights of old, he rode forth to conquer and to do.

But a sudden, sharp, acrid whiff of vapor in his nostrils checked his riotous impulses. It was one thing to ride out to meet the foe, it was another matter when the foe was known to be near. A half mile nearer and the acrid taste in the air turned to a defined veil of smoke, intangible and unreal, at first, which merely seemed to hang about the trunks of the mighty trees and make them seem dim and far away. Nearer yet, and the air grew hard to breathe, the smoke was billowing through the foliage of the pines, which sighed wearily and moaned in a vague fear of the enemy they dreaded most.

A curving gully, too wide to leap, too deep to cross readily, had deflected the boy in his ride until he found himself to the lee of the fire, and the heat of it, oppressive and menacing, assailed him.

Remembering the lay of the land, as he had seen it from his lookout point, Wilbur recalled the fact that no peak or rise was in the vicinity up which he could ride to gain a nearer view of the fire, and he did not dare to ride on and find himself on the windward side of the fire, for then his efforts to hold it back would be unavailing. He rode slowly till he came to the highest tree near. Then, dismounting, Wilbur tied his horse to the foot of the tree, tied him as securely as he knew how, for the animal was snorting in fear at being thus fastened up when the smoke was over his head and the smell of the fire was in his nostrils. Then, buckling on his climbing irons, which he had carried with him that morning because he had thought, if he had time, he might do a little repairing to his telephone line, he started up the side of the great tree. Up and up he went, fifty, sixty, one hundred feet, and still he was not at the top; another twenty feet, and there far above the ground, he rested at last upon a branch whence he could command an outlook upon the forest below.

The fire was near, much nearer than he had imagined, and had he ridden on another ten or fifteen minutes, he might have taken his horse in danger. The blaze was larger than he thought. For half a mile's length, at least, the smoke was rising, and what was beyond he could not rightly see, because the branches of a large tree obscured his sight.

Immediately below him, the little gully, whose curving course had turned him from the straight path, seemed to be the edge of the flames, which had not been able to back up over the water. On this side, clear down to the water's edge the forest floor was burning, but how wide a stretch had been burned over he could not see. Once on the other side of the gully he would be able to judge better what to do.

Below his horse neighed shrilly.

Looking straight down, Wilbur noted a long rolling curl of smoke steal swiftly along the ground a few hundred yards away, and he saw there was no time to lose. Springing from the branch to the trunk of the tree, he started to climb down. But he was over-hurried, and his feet slipped. It was only a foot at most, and Wilbur was not easily frightened, but he turned cold and sick for an instant as he looked below and saw the height from which he so nearly had fallen. Minutes, nay seconds, were precious, but he crawled back upon the branch and sat still a moment to steady his nerves. So startling a shock for so small a slip! He felt thoroughly ashamed of himself, but it had been quite a jolt.

Again the horse neighed, and the fear in the cry was quite unmistakable. Gingerly this time, Wilbur left the kindly support of the branch and made his way down the trunk of the tree, heaving a sigh of profound thankfulness when he reached the ground. His horse looked at him with eyes wild with terror and every muscle atwitch. It was the work of a moment to unfasten the ropes and vault in the saddle, but Wilbur needed all his horsemanship to keep the horse from bolting. Indeed, he did start to run away with the boy, but Wilbur sawed him into a more normal pace and headed him down the gully.

Although the weather had been dry, it seemed that not a few springs must flow above, for there was quite a stream of water, not deep, but rushing very swiftly, and consequently hiding the bottom of the stream. It was no time for looking for a ford, and so, after leading the horse down the bank by the bridle, Wilbur got into the saddle to put the horse across. He would not budge. Every muscle and nerve was tense, and the fire, owing to the curvature of the stream, seeming to come from the other side, the horse refused to move. Wilbur dug in heavily with the spurs. The horse would not move. Again Wilbur used the spurs. Then, snatching the quirt that was fastened on his saddle, the quirt the cattleman had given him after his ride in the cattle stampede, he laid it with all his will across the horse's flanks. Never before, since Wilbur had owned the horse, had he struck him. Frantic, the horse leaped into the stream. It was deeper than the boy had thought, but there was no time to go back, and indeed, unless it was taken at a rush, the horse would not climb the other bank. As they struck the water, therefore, Wilbur rose in his stirrups and lashed the horse a second time. He felt the horse plunge under him, picked him up with the reins as he stumbled on the loose stones in the creek bed and almost fell, and though he was becoming a rider, "hunted leather" by holding on to the pommel of his saddle, as the horse with two or three convulsive lunges climbed like a cat up the opposing bank, and reached the top, trembling in every limb. The gully was crossed.

But there was no time to pause for satisfaction over the crossing of the little stream; that was only the beginning. It would have to be crossed again, higher up, as soon, as they came opposite to the fire. The quirt was still in his hand, and a light touch with it brought the horse to a full gallop. Up along the gully, with the blackened forest floor on the other side, rode Wilbur, until he came to the further end of the fire. It was almost a mile long. Right where the edge of the fire was, with little flames leaping among the needles and the smoke rolling, Wilbur headed the horse for the creek. He expected to have trouble, but the beast had learned his lesson, and went steadily down the creek and over to the other side. The return was in nowise difficult, as it was on the side opposite the fire that the bank was steep. Hastily Wilbur tied up his horse on the burned-out area, seized his shovel, and started along the line of the fire, beating it out with the flat of his shovel where the flames were small, then going to lee of it he made a firebreak by turning up a narrow line of earth.

His hands began to blister and his lips grew so parched that he could endure it no longer, and snatched a moment to go back to the stream and lave his face and hands. He took off his coat, dipped it in the water, and came with it all dripping to beat out the fire with that. Foot by foot and yard by yard he worked his way along the line, every once in a while running back over the part he had already beaten to make sure that all was out. The afternoon was drawing on and for about a quarter of a mile the fire was entirely out, and for another quarter it was almost under control.

Madly the boy worked, his breath coming in gasps, his lungs aching from the smoke, so that it became agony even to breathe, the ground hot beneath his feet, and his feet beginning to blister, as his hands had done an hour before, but there was no let-up. He had come to fight fire, and he would fight fire. Another mad hour's battle, not so successfully, and, contrary to the usual custom, the wind began to rise at sunset; it might die down in a couple of hours, but in the meantime damage might be done.

Little by little the shadows grew deeper, and before it got entirely dark Wilbur tried, but vainly, to reach the end of the line, for he knew well that if a night wind rose and got a hold upon the remnant of the fire that remained all his work would go for nothing. With all his might he ran to the far end of the line, determining to work from that end up to meet the area where he had conquered. Foot by foot he gained, but no longer was he able to work along a straight line, the gusts of wind, here and there, sweeping through the trees had fanned stretches, perhaps only a few yards wide, but had driven them forward a hundred feet. But as it grew darker the wind began to fall again, though with the darkness the red glow of the burning needles and the flames of the burning twigs showed more luridly and made it seem more terrifying. Still he gained headway, foot after foot jealously contesting the battle with the fire and the wind.

So short a space remaining, and though he seemed too tired and sore to move, still his shovel worked with never a pause, still he scraped away all that would burn from the path of a little line of flame. The line of flame grew shorter, but even as he looked a gust came along, which swept a tongue of fire fifty yards at a breath. Wilbur rushed after it, knowing the danger of these side-way fires, but before that gust had lulled the tongue of fire reached a little clearing which the boy had not known was there, only a rod or two of grass, but that browned by the sun and the drought until it seemed scarcely more than tinder. If it should touch that!

Despite the fact that his shoes were dropping from his feet, the leather being burned through, Wilbur sped after the escaping fire. He reached it. But as he reached, he heard the needles rustle overhead and saw the branches sway. As yet the breeze had not touched the ground, but before two strokes with the wet coat had been made, the last of the gusts of the evening wind struck him. It caught the little tongue of flame Wilbur had so manfully striven to overtake, swept it out upon the clearing, and almost before the boy could realize that his chance was gone, the grass was a sheet of flame and the fire had entered the forest beyond in a dozen places.

Wilbur was but a boy after all, and sick and heart-broken, he had to swallow several times very hard to keep from breaking down. And the reaction and fatigue together stunned him into inertness. For a moment only, then his persistent stubbornness came to the front.

"That fire's got to be put out," he said aloud, "as the Chief Forester said, back in Washington, if it takes the whole State to do it."

He walked back to his horse and started for his little cabin home. How he reached there, Wilbur never rightly knew. He felt like a traitor, leaving the fire still burning which he had tried so hard to conquer, but he knew he had done all he could. As he rode home, however, he saw through the trees another gleam, and taking out his glasses, saw in the distance a second fire, in no way connected with that which he had fought. This cheered him up greatly, for he felt that he could rightly call for help for two fires without any reflection on his courage or his grit, where he hated to tell that he had tried and failed to put out a blaze which perhaps an older or a stronger man might have succeeded in quelling. He called up the Ranger.

"Rifle-Eye," he said over the 'phone as soon as he got a response, "there's a fire here that looks big. In fact, there's two. I've been after one all afternoon, and I nearly got it under, but when the wind rose it got away from me. And there seems to be a bigger one pretty close to it."

"Well, son, I s'pose you're needin' help," came the reply.

"All hands, I think," said the boy. "By the time I can get back there the two fires probably will have joined, and the blaze will be several miles long."

"Surest thing you know," said the Ranger. "Where do you locate these fires?"

Wilbur described with some detail the precise point where the fires were raging.

"You'd better get back on the job," said Rifle-Eye promptly, "and try an' hold it down the best you can. I'll have some one there on the jump. We want to get it under to-night, as it's a lot easier 'n in the daytime."

Never did the little tent look so inviting or so cozy to Wilbur as that moment. But he had his orders. "Get back on the job," the Ranger had said. He took the time to change his shoes and to snatch up some cold grub which was easy to get. But he ate it standing, not daring to sit down lest he should go to sleep—and go to sleep when he had been ordered out! He ate standing. Then, going down to the corral, he saddled Kit.

He rode quietly up past the tent.

"I guess," he said, "I really never did want to go to bed so much before, but—" he turned Kit's head to the trail.

It was well for Wilbur that he had ridden the other horse that day, for Kit was fresh and ready. The moon had risen and was nearly full, but Wilbur shivered as much from nervousness and responsibility as from fatigue. It was useless for him to try riding at any high rate of speed in the uncertain light, and in any case, the boy felt that his labors for a half an hour more or less would not mean as much as when it had been a question of absolutely extinguishing a small blaze. Kit danced a little in the fresh night air, but Wilbur sat so heavily and listlessly upon her back that the mare sensed something wrong and constantly turned her wise face round to see.

"I'm just tired, Kit," said the boy to her, "that's all. Don't get gay to-night; I'm not up to it."

And the little mare, as though she had understood every word, settled down to a quiet lope down the trail. How far he had ridden or in what direction he was traveling Wilbur at last became entirely unconscious, for, utterly worn out, he had fallen asleep in the saddle, keeping his seat merely by instinct and owing to the gentle, easy pace of his mare.

He was wakened by a heavy hand being put upon his shoulder, and rousing himself with a start, he found the grave, kindly eyes of the old Ranger gleaming on him in the moonlight.

"Sleeping, son?" queried the old mountaineer.

"Yes, Rifle-Eye, I guess I must have been," said the lad, "just dozed off. I'm dog-tired. I've been on that fire all afternoon."

The Ranger looked at him keenly.

"Best thing you could have done," he said. "You'll feel worse for a few minutes, an' then you'll find that cat-nap is just as good as a whole night's sleep. That is," he added, "it is for a while. What's the fire like? I tried to get somethin' out of Ben, but he was actin' queerly, an' I left him alone. But he seemed to know pretty well where it was."

Wilbur tried to explain the story of the fire, but his tale soon became incoherent, and before they had ridden another half a mile, his story had died down to a few mutterings and he was asleep again. The old hunter rode beside him, his hand ready to catch him should he waver in the saddle, but Kit loped along at her easiest gait and the boy scarcely moved. Rifle-Eye woke him again when they left the trail and broke into the forest.

"I reckon you better wake up, son," he said, "landin' suddenly on your head on a rock is some abrupt as an alarm clock."

Wilbur dropped the reins to stretch himself.

"I feel a lot better now," he announced, "just as good as ever. Except for my hands," he added ruefully, as returning wakefulness brought back with it the consciousness of smart and hurt, "and my feet are mighty sore, too. We're right near the fire, too, aren't we," he continued. "Gee, that was nifty sleeping nearly all the way. I guess I must have felt you were around, Rifle-Eye, and so I slept easily, knowing it would come out all right with you here."

"I ain't never been famous for hypnotizin' any forest fire that I've heard of," said the old hunter, smiling, "but I've got a lurkin' idea somewhere that we'll get this headed off all right. An' in any case, there ain't much folks livin' in the path of the fire, if the wind keeps the way she is now."

Wilbur thought for a moment over the lay of the land and the direction in which the flames were moving.

"There's the mill," he said suddenly and excitedly.

"Yes, son," said the old hunter. "I'd been thinkin' of that. There's the mill."

CHAPTER XVI
IN THE MIDST OF A SEA OF FIRE

A subdued but fiery inspiration, as of some monster breathing deeply in the darkness, gradually made itself heard above the voices of the night, and an eddying gust brought from the distance the sound of twigs and branches crackling as they burned. As yet the fire was not visible, save for the red-bronze glow seen through the trees reflected on the sky above. But before they reached the scene of the fire, Wilbur realized how different it was from the blaze he had left. Then it was a difficulty to be overcome: now, it was a peril to be faced.

"It has run about three miles since I left it," Wilbur said. "I hope we're not too late."

"It's never too late to try, son," replied the Ranger, "so long as there is a tree left unburned. There ain't anything in life that it ever gets too late to try over. If a thing's done, it ain't too late ever to try to do something else which will make up for the first, is it?"

"But I failed to stop it before," said Wilbur.

"Nary a fail. A fight ain't lost until it's over. An' when this little scrap is over the fire'll be out. You ain't had but one round with this fire so far."

"That's certainly some fire," rejoined the boy as they turned sharply from a glade to the edge of a hill that looked upon the forest just below. It was a sight of fear. Overhead, the clouds flying before the wind were alternately revealing and hiding the starlit and moonlit sky behind, the dark and ragged wisps of storm-scud seeming to fly in panic from what they saw below them. The wind moaned as though enchained and forced to blow by some tyrannic power, instead of swaying before the breeze, the needles of the pines seemed to tremble and shudder in the blast, and dominating the whole, — somber, red, and malevolent, — the fire engulfed the forest floor. In the distance, where some dead timber had been standing, the flames had crept up the trunks of the trees, and now fanned by the gusts of wind, were beginning to run amid the tops.

"Will it be a crown-fire, Rifle-Eye?" asked Wilbur, remembering what he had heard of the fearful devastation committed by a fire when once it secured a violent headway among the pines.

"It's in the tops now," said the old hunter, pointing with his finger, "but I don't reckon there's enough wind yet to hold it up there. The worst of it is that it's not long to morning now, an' we shall lose the advantage o' fightin' it at night. I reckon we'd better get down and see what we can do."

In a few minutes the hunter and Wilbur had fastened their horses and presently were beside the fire. To the boy's surprise the old hunter made no attack upon the fire itself, but, going in advance of it some hundred feet, with the boy's hoe, which he dragged after him like a plow, made a furrow in the earth almost as rapidly as a man could walk. This, Wilbur, with ax and shovel, widened. The old hunter never seemed to stop once, but, however curving and twisting his course might be, the boy noted that the furrow invariably occurred at the end of a stretch where few needles had fallen on the ground and the débris was very scant.

After about a mile of this, the hunter curved his furrow sharply in toward the burned-out portion, ending his line behind the line of fire. He then sent Wilbur back along the line he had just traversed to insure that none of the fire had crossed the guard thus made. Then, starting about twenty feet from the curve on the fire-guard, he took another wide curve in front of the floor-fire, favoring the place where the needles lay thinnest, until he came to a ridge. Following him, Wilbur noted that the old woodsman had made no attempt to stop the fire on the upward grade, but had apparently left it to the mercy of the fire, whereas, on the further side of the ridge, where the fire would have to burn down, the old hunter had made but a very scanty fire-guard. Then Wilbur remembered that he had been told it was easy to stop a fire when it was running down a hill, and he realized that if, in the beginning, instead of actually endeavoring to put out the fire, he had made a wide circuit around it, and by utilizing those ridges, he could have held the fire to the spot where it began. For a moment this nearly broke him all up, until he remembered that he had seen another fire, and that Rifle-Eye had told him of a third one yet.

Wilbur was working doggedly, yet in a spiritless, tired fashion, beating out the fire with a wet gunnysack as it reached the fire-guard of the old hunter's making, and very carefully putting out any spark that the wind drove across it, working almost without thought. But as he topped the ridge and came within full view of the fire that had started among the tops, his listlessness fell from him. Against the glow he could see the outline of the figure of the hunter, and he ran up to him.

"It's all out, back there," he panted. "What shall we do here?"

For the first time the Ranger seemed to have no answer ready. Then he said slowly:

"I reckon we can hold this bit of it, up yonder on the mountain, but there's a line of fire runnin' around by the gully, and the wind's beginnin' a-howlin' through there. I don't reckon we can stop that. We may have to fall back beyond the river. We'll need axmen, now. You've got a good mare; ride down to Pete's mine and bring all hands. The government will pay them, an' they'll come. There's the dawn; it'll be light in half an hour. You'd better move, too."

Wilbur started off at a shambling run, half wondering, as he did so, how it was he was able to keep up at all. But as he looked back he saw the old hunter, ax on shoulder, going quietly up the hill into the very teeth of the fire to head it off on the mountain top, if he could. He reached Kit and climbed into the saddle. But he was not sleepy, though almost too weary to sit upright. One moment the forest would be light as a glare from the fire reached him, the next moment it would be all the darker for the contrast. For a mile he rode over the blackened and burned forest floor, some trees still ablaze and smoking. Every step he took, for all he knew, might be leading him on into a fire-encircled place from which he would have difficulty in escaping, but on he went. There was no trail, he only had a vague sense of direction, and on both sides of him was fire. Probably fire was also in front, and if so he was riding into it, but he had his orders and on he must go. The mine, he knew, was lower down on the gully, and so roughly he followed it. Twice he had to force Kit to cross, but it was growing light now, so the little mare took the water quietly and followed the further bank. Suddenly he heard horses' hoofs, evidently a party, and he shouted. An answering shout was the response, and the horses pulled up. He touched Kit and in a minute or two broke through to them.

"Oh, it's you, Mr. Merritt," said the boy, "I was just wondering who it might be."

"The fire's over there," said the Supervisor. "What are you doing here?"

"Rifle-Eye sent me to get the men at Pete's mine," he said.

"They're here," replied the Forest Chief. "How's the fire?"

"Bad," said the boy. "Rifle-Eye said he thought we would have to fall back beyond the river."

"Don't want to," said Merritt, "there's a lot of good timber between here and the river."

"Nothin' to it," said one of the miners. "Unless the wind shifts, it's an easy gamble she goes over the river and don't notice it none."

The Supervisor put his horse to the gallop, followed by the party, all save one miner, who, familiar with the country, led the way, finding some trail utterly undistinguishable to the rest. Seeing the vantage point, as Rifle-Eye had done, he made for the crest of the hill.

"Any chances?" asked the Supervisor.

"I reckon not," said Rifle-Eye. "You can't hold it here; there's a blaze down over yonder and another below the hill."

"Who set that fire?" said Merritt suddenly. Wilbur jumped. It had not occurred to him that the fire could have started in any other manner than by accident, and indeed he had not thought of its cause at all.

The old Ranger looked quietly at his superior officer.

"It's allers mighty hard to tell where a fire started after it's once got a-going," he said, "and it's harder to tell who set it a-going."

"I want to stop it at the river."

The old woodsman shook his head.

"You ain't got much chance," he said; "I reckon at the ridge on the other side of the river you can hold her, but she's crept along the gully an' she'll just go a-whoopin' up the hill. I wouldn't waste any time at the river."

"But there's the mill!"

"We ain't no ways to blame because Peavey Jo built his mill in front of a fire. An', anyhow, the mill's in the middle of a clearing."

The Supervisor frowned.

"His mill is on National Forest land, and we ought to try and save it," he said.

"I'm goin' clear to the ridge," remarked the Ranger, "an' I reckon you-all had better, too. I ain't achin' none to see the mill burn, but I'd as lieve it was Peavey Jo's as any one else."

"I'd like to know," Merritt repeated, "who set that fire."

The Ranger made no answer, but walked off to where his horse was tethered and rode away. The other party without a moment's delay struck off to the trail leading to the mill. The distance was not great, but Wilbur had lost all count of time. It seemed to him that he had either been fighting fire or riding at high speed through luridly lighted forest glades for years and years, and that it would never stop.

At the mill they found a wild turmoil of excitement. All the hands were at work, most of them wetting down the lumber, while other large piles which were close to the edge of the forest were being moved out of danger. The horses all had been taken from the stables, and the various sheds and buildings were being thoroughly soaked. The big mill engine was throbbing, lines of hose playing in every direction, for although the timber around the mill had been cleared as much as possible, negligence had been shown in permitting some undergrowth to spring up unchecked. Owing to the conformation of the land, too, the bottom on which the mill stood was smaller than customary.

In the early morning light the great form of Peavey Jo seemed to assume giant proportions. He was here, there, and everywhere at the moment, and his blustering voice could be heard bellowing out orders, which, to do him justice, were the best possible. As soon as the Supervisor and his party appeared he broke out into a violent tirade against them for not keeping a fit watch over the forest and allowing a fire to get such a headway on a night when in the evening there had been so little wind, whereas now a gale was rising fast. But Merritt did not waste breath in reply; he simply ordered his men to get in and do all they could to insure the safety of the mill.

Wilbur, who had been set at cutting out the underbrush, found that his strength was about played out. Once, indeed, he shouldered his ax and started to walk back to say that he could do no more, but before he reached the place where his chief was working his determination returned, and he decided to go back and work till he dropped right there. He had given up bothering about his hands and feet being so blistered and sore, for all such local pain was dulled by the utter collapse of nerve-sensation. He couldn't think clearly enough to think that he was feeling pain; he could not think at all. He had been told to cut brush and he did so as a machine, working automatically, but seeing nothing and hearing nothing of what was going on around him.

Presently an animal premonition of fear struck him as he became conscious of a terrific wave of heat, and he could hear in the distance the roar of the flames coming closer. Raging through the resinous pine branches the blaze had swept fiercely around the side of the hill. As the boy looked up he could see it suddenly break into greater vigor as the up-draft on the hill fanned it to a wilder fury and made a furnace of the place where he had been standing with Merritt and Rifle-Eye scarcely more than an hour before.

Meanwhile the wind drove the flames steadily onward toward the threatened mill. It was becoming too hot for any human being to stay where Wilbur was, but the boy seemed to have lost the power of thought. He chopped and chopped like a machine, not noticing, indeed, not being able to notice that he was toiling there alone. It grew hotter and hotter, his breath came in quick, short gasps, and each breath hurt his lungs cruelly as he breathed the heat into them, but he worked on as in a dream. Suddenly he felt his shoulder seized. It was the Supervisor, who twisted him round and, pointing to the little bridge across the river which spanned the stream just above the mill, he shouted:

"Run!"

But the boy's spirit was too exhausted to respond, though he got into a dog trot and started for the bridge. Perilous though every second's delay was, Merritt would not go ahead of the boy, though he could have outdistanced his shambling and footsore pace two to one, but kept beside him urging and threatening him alternately. The fire was on their heels, but they were in the clearing. On the bridge one of the miners was standing, riding the fastest horse in the party, holding, and with great difficulty holding, in hand the horse of the Supervisor and the boy's mare, Kit. Their very clothes were smoking as they reached the bridge.

Suddenly, a huge, twisted tree, full of sap, which stood on the edge of the clearing, exploded with a crash like a cannon, and a flaming branch, twenty feet in length, hurtled itself over their heads and fell full on the further side of the bridge, barring their way. Upon the narrow bridge the horses reared in a sudden panic and tried to bolt, but the miner was an old-time cowboy, and he held them in hand. Merritt helped the lad into the saddle before mounting himself. But even in that moment the bridge began to smoke, and in less than a minute the whole structure would be ablaze. The miner dug his heels, spurred, into the sides of his horse, and the animal in fear and desperation leaped over the hissing branch that lay upon the bridge. The Supervisor's horse and Kit followed suit. As they landed on the other side, however, the head of the forest reined in for a moment, and looking round, shouted suddenly:

"The mill!"

Wilbur pulled in Kit. So far as could be seen, none of the forest fire had reached the mill; the sparks which had fallen upon the roof had gone out harmlessly, so thoroughly had the place been soaked, yet through the door of the mill the flames could be seen on the inside. At first Wilbur thought it must be some kind of a reflection. But as they watched, Peavey Jo rode up.

He had crossed the bridge earlier, and was on the safe side of the river watching his mill.

Suddenly, from out the door of the mill, outlined clearly against the fire within, came an ungainly, shambling figure. The features could not be seen, but the gait was unmistakable. He came running in an odd, loose-jointed fashion toward the bridge. But just before he reached it the now blazing timbers burned through and the bridge crashed into the stream.

"It's Ben," muttered Wilbur confusedly; "I guess I've got to go back," and he headed Kit for the trail.

But the Supervisor leaned over and almost crushed the bones of the boy's hand in his restraining grip.

"No need," he said, "he's all right now."

For as he spoke Wilbur saw Ben leap from the bank on the portion of the burned bridge which had collapsed on his side of the stream. A few quick strokes with the ax the boy was carrying and the timbers were free, and crouched down upon them the boy was being carried down the stream. His peril was extreme, for below as well as above the fire was sweeping down on either side of the mill, and it was a question of minutes, almost of seconds, whether the bridge-raft would pass down the river before the fire struck or whether it would be caught.

"If the wind would only lull!" ejaculated the boy.

"I'll stay here till I see him burn," replied Peavey Jo grimly.

But Wilbur's wish met its fulfillment, for just for the space that one could count ten the wind slackened, and every second meant a few yards of safety to the half-witted lad. Though they were risking their lives by staying, the three men waited, waited as still as they could for the fear of their horses, until the boy disappeared round a curve of the river. A muttered execration from Peavey Jo announced the lad's safety. It angered the usually calm Supervisor.

"That ends you," he said. "You're licked, and you know it. Your mill's gone, your timber's gone, and your credit's gone. Don't let me see you on this forest again."

"You think I do no more, eh? Me, I forget? Non! By and by you remember Peavey Jo. Now I ride down river. That boy, you see him? He see the sun rise this morning. He no see the sun set. No. Nor ever any more. I follow the river trail. I do not say good-by, like the old song," he added, scowling his fury; "you wish yes! Non! I say au revoir, and perhaps sooner than you t'ink."

He wheeled and turned down the river. The Supervisor turned to the miner.

"It's not my business to stop him," he said, "and the boy's got the start. He can't reach there before the fire does, now."

Then, as though regretting the lull, the wind shrieked with a new and more vindictive fury, as though it saw its vengeance before it. Almost at a breath it seemed the whole body of flame appeared to lift itself to the skies and then fall like a devouring fury upon the forest on the hither side of the river below, whither Peavey Jo had ridden.

In the distance the two men heard a horse scream, and they knew. But Wilbur did not hear.

They had waited almost too long, for the wind, rising to its greatest height, had carried the fire above them almost to the edge of the river, and now there was no question about its crossing. Further delay meant to be hemmed in by a ring of fire. With a shout the miner slackened the reins and his horse leaped into a gallop, after him Merritt, and the boy close behind. Wilbur had ridden fast before, but never had he known such speed as now. The trail was clear before them to the top of the ridge, the fire was behind, and the wind was hurling masses of flames about them on every side. The horses fled with the speed of fear, and the Supervisor drew a breath of relief as they crossed a small ridge below the greater ridge whither they were bound.

Once a curl of flame licked clear over their heads and ignited a tree in front of them, but they were past it again before it caught fair hold. The boy could feel Kit's flanks heaving as she drew her breath hard, and with the last instinct of safety he threw away everything that he carried, even the fire-fighting tools being released. Only another mile, but the grade was fearfully steep, the steeper the harder for the horses but the better for the fire. Kit stumbled. A little less than a mile left! He knew she could not do it.

179

The mare had been kept astretch all night, and her heart was breaking under the strain. Any second she might fall.

The trail curved. And round the curve, with three horses saddled and waiting, sat the old Ranger, facing the onrush of the fire as imperturbably as though his own life were in no way involved. The miner's horse was freshest and he reached the group first. As he did so, he swung out of his saddle, was on one of the three and off. The riderless horse, freed from the burden, followed up the trail. Merritt and Wilbur reached almost at the same time.

"I reckon," drawled Rifle-Eye, "that's a pretty close call."

"He's done," said the Supervisor, ignoring the remark. "Toss him up."

With a speed that seemed almost incredible to any one accustomed to his leisurely movements, the old Ranger dismounted, picked Wilbur bodily out of the saddle, set him on one of the fresh animals, freed Kit, mounted himself, and was off in less than thirty seconds. For the first half mile it was touch and go, for the trail was steep and even the three fresh horses found the pace terrific. But little by little the timber thinned and the fire gained less hold. Then, with a burst they came into a clearing along the top of the ridge. The crest was black with workers, over two hundred men were there, and on every side was to be heard the sound of trees crashing to the ground, most of them by dynamite.

Where the head of the trail reached the crest stood the doctor and his wife, the "little white lady" trembling with excitement as she watched the fearful race from the jaws of a fiery death. The doctor plucked Wilbur from his saddle as the horse rushed by him. The boy's senses were reeling, but before he sank into insensibility from fatigue he heard Merritt say:

"Loyle, when you're a Ranger next year, I want you on my forest."

THE END